Alex was stunned.

"You'v _____ ?"

He didn't know  med
pretty cold to hi   arry
him off to some   ow,
he had thought /   Well,
it was nonsense,

"I'm sure she won't do," Alex said with as much dignity
as he could manage. "Now, if you'll excuse me, I need to
go write some prescriptions."

He walked down to the exam room and closed the door.

He was finally interested in a woman, and she was
trying to match him up with someone else. Of course, it
was probably for the best. He was leaving in a few weeks
anyway. And, just because he was interested in her,
didn't mean he had anything to offer someone like that.

Books by Janet Tronstad

Steeple Hill Love Inspired

*An Angel for Dry Creek
*A Gentleman for Dry Creek
*A Bride for Dry Creek
*A Rich Man for Dry Creek
*A Hero for Dry Creek
*A Baby for Dry Creek
*A Dry Creek Christmas
*Sugar Plums for Dry Creek
*At Home in Dry Creek
**The Sisterhood of the Dropped Stitches
*A Match Made in Dry Creek
*Shepherds Abiding in Dry Creek
**A Dropped Stitches Christmas
*Dry Creek Sweethearts
**A Heart for the Dropped Stitches
*A Dry Creek Courtship
*Snowbound in Dry Creek
**A Dropped Stitches Wedding
*Small-Town Brides
   "A Dry Creek Wedding"
*Silent Night in Dry Creek
*Wife Wanted in Dry Creek
Doctor Right

Steeple Hill
Love Inspired Historical

*Calico Christmas
   at Dry Creek
*Mistletoe Courtship
   "Christmas Bells for
      Dry Creek"

*Dry Creek
**The Sisterhood of the Dropped Stitches

JANET TRONSTAD

grew up on a farm in central Montana, spending many winter days reading books about the Old West and the gold rush days of Alaska. During college she got a chance to see the beauty of Alaska for herself when she worked a summer on Kodiak Island in a salmon factory, packing fish eggs for a Japanese firm. Because of those experiences, she is excited to be part of this series. Janet lives in Pasadena, California, where she writes full-time when not dreaming of other places.

Doctor Right
Janet Tronstad

Steeple
Hill®

Published by Steeple Hill Books™

Special thanks and acknowledgment to Janet Tronstad for her contribution to the Alaskan Bride Rush miniseries.

STEEPLE HILL BOOKS

Steeple
Hill®

Recycling programs
for this product may
not exist in your area.

ISBN-13: 978-0-373-81498-5

DOCTOR RIGHT

Copyright © 2010 by Harlequin Books S.A.

www.SteepleHill.com

Printed in U.S.A.

I will lift up mine eyes unto the hills, from whence cometh my help. My help cometh from the Lord, which made heaven and earth.

—*Psalms* 121:1–2

This book is dedicated to my friends in the Love Inspired Historical discussion group on Goodreads. We've taken many exotic trips together in our minds and I hope they'll love this one to Alaska, too.

Chapter One

If she opened the clinic door, Maryann Jenner knew a gust of cold wind would blow inside that would smell of wood smoke, mostly from the stovepipes jutting up from the row of flat and peaked roofs that lined the main road into Treasure Creek, Alaska. As much as she liked the scent, not all of the patients did, so she left the door closed and instead looked out the window at the rugged, green mountains that edged the backside of this small tourist town. She still couldn't believe she was working in this postcard-perfect place.

For the first time in her twenty-six years, she was beginning to feel like she had a chance at the peaceful life she wanted. She'd been an unwilling participant in other people's dramas—mostly her parent's—since she was born. Now she was far enough away that she could love her mother and father without being dragged into the soap operas that were their respective, disconnected lives. As though to celebrate her new life, she'd landed the perfect job, working with the ever so perfect Dr. Alex Havens in this perfect little clinic in paradise.

"Oh, no," she muttered to herself and took a quick glance over her shoulder to be sure the doctor was still in the back room examining six-year-old Johnny Short's ear infection. She had a bad habit of actually believing what she conjured up in her day dreams when looking out that window. Treasure Creek was wonderful, of course, but the pediatrician could be, she had to admit, a bit demanding at times. And particular. And downright testy about some things. He'd even been dubbed The Ice Man by her predecessor. And, since Maryann was now his nurse, it was apparently her job to make his days run smoothly.

Ordinarily, that wasn't much of a problem. She was good at maintaining order. Besides, the doctor might be an ice man around adults, but children seemed to love him, and since they were his patients, everything moved along fine in their small clinic. She and Alex had figured out how to work together.

But if the line of women marching up the

slight hill toward them were the ones she thought they were, she was going to earn her salary today. The final thing he'd asked before hiring her last month was if she knew how to keep the fancy women away. She'd assured him she did, even though she was new in town and hadn't known what—or who—he was talking about.

Today she knew. Several months ago, *Now Woman* magazine had run an article on the bachelor tour guides in Treasure Creek, and before Maryann arrived, women had started swarming up here in hot pursuit of husbands. The locals called them fancy women because they looked like exotic tropical birds when set against the sturdy, practical dress of the local people.

Maryann had never heard of the women attacking their target all together, though. Not like this. Alex was only a part-time guide with Alaska's Treasures tour company, earning just one brief mention in the article.

Of course, he was completely single and unattached. But—oh, dear.

The door flew open before Maryann had time to retreat. The smell of perfume followed the women inside, along with a surprising number of the rather large mosquitoes Alaska is famous for. She wasn't sure if it was the heavy floral scents that attracted these insects so late in the season, or if it was the red shine on the women's lips and nails. Either way, the fact that the women didn't complain about the bites they must be getting only proved how determined they were to be here.

"This is a pe-dia-tric clinic," Maryann raised herself up to her full five-foot-seven-inches and announced in her strictest nurse voice. "Adult patients need to go down the street to Dr. Logan's clinic."

She'd worked on that voice in her nurse's training, until it could silence a group of rowdy boys. It didn't even stop the women from chattering long enough for them to really listen to her. Of course, part of that could be because they were reaching up to try and tame their windblown hair.

"I have full-coverage insurance, so any doctor will see me." A showy blonde, with a dandelion head of bleached hair and the plumpest purple lips Maryann had ever seen, sat down in one of the few adult chairs in the waiting room and crossed her nylon-encased legs in a theatrical gesture. Then she looked at Maryann. "It was part of my last divorce settlement. The doctor can do any test he wants on me. My ex will cover it if the insurance doesn't, so the doctor doesn't need to worry about the bill being paid."

"I just need a prescription refill," a young waif-like woman whispered as she slipped into one of the nearby children's chairs. She had long brown hair and a slight overbite. "Do you know if the doctor likes to walk on the beach in the moonlight? I adore the beach. Not the Alaskan beach, of course—it's too rocky and cold—but, you know, the regular beach."

The wind had ruffled the young woman and she nervously tried to pull her tangled hair into place.

"I can't—" Maryann said, her voice rising slightly. She looked around. Eight women were in the room. None of them looked sick, especially since the cold outside had given their cheeks higher than normal color. Besides, together they were wearing enough gold jewelry to open a pawn shop. They had marched up here in full battle armor. But why had they come, now of all times—on this cold, blustery day?

And then the realization hit her and she felt a twist in the pit of her stomach. It was her fault. She'd told her cousin last night how much his young patients would miss Alex after his contract expired at the end of the month.

Her cousin remarked that if she wanted the man to stay in Treasure Creek, she needed to get him happily married to a local woman. Which led to the unfortunate remark by her that no woman with warm blood flowing through her veins would marry The Ice Man. Which led to her cousin saying that there was a match for everyone and Maryann could find someone for the doctor if she put her mind to it. After all, her cousin added, Maryann was good at managing other people's romances— hadn't her parents relied on her to help them find their next soul mates? And the ones after that?

Unfortunately, she and her newly-engaged cousin, Karenna, had been eating hamburgers in Lizbet's Diner when they'd had their conversation. Someone must have overheard. Gossip traveled fast in a small town like this, and it often got twisted. Maryann knew she shouldn't have said anything about Alex. And worst of all, she had taken a guess at a woman who might suit him, and, even though it wasn't one of the fancy women, the whole thing must have resulted in today's sudden invasion.

"I'm sorry, but you'll have to leave," Maryann said, as she tried to herd the women to the door. They weren't budging. She didn't suppose she could call 911 over something like this. "The doctor is in the exam room with a patient and—"

"He can be my doctor any time," a woman with bouncy, copper ringlets said, as she wiggled out of Maryann's herd, walked over to a chair and sat down looking pleased with herself.

The fancy women all giggled.

Why did people seeking romance all become silly as teenagers, Maryann wondered. She raised her voice. "What I'm trying to say is that there are no appointments left for today."

She hoped that would do it.

"Or tomorrow either," she added quickly just in case. "We're all booked."

She really liked this job; she didn't want to be fired. Alex had promised to give her a good recommendation to his replacement. Well, it would be his temporary replacement. The agency had already said they could only send someone to fill in for a few months while they kept looking for a new scholarship doctor to take over the clinic for another three years. If they couldn't find someone, they would close the clinic in six months.

Why did it all have to be so complicated? The children here needed a doctor. And Maryann didn't want to lose her job and return to the lower forty-eight. The obvious solution was to have Alex put down roots here in Treasure Creek. Of course, he'd have to want to stay. Her cousin was right about a wife being the answer, but—despite her earlier comments about him being The Ice Man—Maryann knew full well he could have his pick of brides. Some women would tell themselves he would thaw eventually; others might not care.

No, he would be the one who was hard to please when it came to marriage. The nurse before her claimed Alex hadn't dated anyone in the time she'd known him. All he cared about was that clinic he was going to build in Los Angeles.

"I'm Delilah Carrington. I'm sure he'll see me," the copper ringlet woman said as she gave a grand wave with an arm wrapped in thin gold bracelets. Then she looked around and slowly frowned. "I would think a doctor's office would be better equipped though. This place is a little old and scruffy, isn't it?"

She made it sound as though the patients regularly stuck their old chewing gum under the chairs bottoms, Maryann thought—which she was sure they did not, since she'd checked a time or two.

"He's a scholarship doctor," another of the

women said, as though that explained any shabbiness. "You know, the government pays for him to go to medical school and he has to work in a place like this for a few years to pay them back. All the poor kids do it."

Maryann bristled at the implication that because Alex didn't have money, somehow that made him less of a success. He was a brilliant doctor. She'd known that after working the first day for him. Plus, he really cared about his little patients. He even treated the children from the Taiya Village, part of the Tlingit tribe, for free. If the town got another scholarship doctor, he probably wouldn't go out to the village at all. It was extra work, and not part of the agreement the doctors signed. That was another reason she wanted Alex to stay on here. The Tlingit kids needed him as much as the kids in Treasure Creek did, and probably more.

"The city owns this clinic," Maryann said firmly. "The place is charming and very neatly organized. It might be a little scratched up, but we keep it very clean. Besides, Dr. Havens knows all of the latest treatments."

The room was quiet as the women looked around. Apparently, they'd been surprised enough at that declaration to listen.

"What kind of treatments?" one of the

women asked, looking around the office dubiously. "Those herbal things?"

"Medical treatments," Maryann snapped back. She saw no reason to admit that he studied the native remedies of the Tlingit people. She'd already said too much about the man last night. "They're the kind any good, well-trained doctor uses. Some from the Mayo Clinic."

Then she scowled at the women, daring any of them to make more remarks about this building or the doctor who ran it. The clinic was set in one of the restored log cabins that were left over from the original gold rush prospectors who had founded this town in 1897. She'd like to see how these fancy women would have stood up a hundred years from now. Besides, people should be proud to use this place, she told herself; it had solid history.

The town had taken ownership of the cabin decades ago, renting it out to a souvenir shop for years until someone decided they needed a children's clinic in town. They widened the doorway and added a side ramp off the porch for wheelchairs, and the cabin became a clinic. Except for the thickly lacquered logs, the only other holdover from its tourist days was Horace, the slightly droopy moose head hanging over the door.

"So this means our doctor is poor," Delilah finally said in the silence, that same frown on her face. "If he had to have a scholarship, I mean. That can't be good. Does he have any money at all?"

"Honey, a man with looks like Dr. Havens doesn't need money," another of the women—Joleen something—declared with a warm chuckle. The woman was wearing a spandex jumpsuit in a leopard print and spiked black heels. A long gold chain hung around her neck, and somehow she'd managed to get her blond hair rearranged after the wind. "Besides, he's not going to stay poor. He's a doctor. He'll be rich before you know it, especially since he's going back to Los Angeles. You should see the expensive cars men like him drive down there."

That started the rest of the women talking about the doctor again. And they weren't just talking about his money.

Maryann didn't need to hear the women to know what they were saying. Alex was tall, dark and handsome—she'd be the first to admit it. Any woman who sighed over Rhett Butler—and she had a feeling most of those women in the waiting room had—would be drawn to the good doctor. He had that same kind of jaw. Plus, he had strong biceps, a chin with a dimple—just like they said, and with all the glowing adjectives they used. It was amazing that the fancy women had taken this long to fill up the man's waiting room.

The more they talked, the gloomier Maryann got. Until last night, she'd found working with Alex companionable enough that she'd almost forgotten he was drop-dead gorgeous. Years ago, she'd vowed never to trust a handsome man. Assuming that vow still held, her cousin had made the criticism rather loudly last night over dinner that, because of it, Maryann might be a little bit unfair to her employer when she called him The Ice Man. Everyone deserved a chance to prove himself, her cousin said; maybe Maryann needed to get to know him better. Besides, no boss was perfect.

Which reminded Maryann, if she wanted to keep him as her boss, she needed to warn him about these women, and quickly.

"Let me go see how long the doctor will be," she announced casually as she started toward the back exam room. There was a good-size window on the side wall. It was a bit of a drop to the ground, but Alex was in excellent physical shape. At least the fancy women had gotten that much right.

If she hadn't been looking straight at the door, Maryann wouldn't have seen the knob turn. She formed her lips and called out, "Nooo."

But it was too late. Her voice came out thin and the door opened anyway. Johnny Short walked out with his mother. Both of them looked surprised at the crowded waiting room.

"Isn't he cute?" a brunette with diamond clips in her hair and gold chains on her ankles said, as she stood up and beamed at the wide-eyed little boy. She tugged on her V-neck sweater, which only made more skin show. "Aren't you a sweetie?"

The diamond woman took a step toward the boy before his mother put up a hand to stop her. "He's only six and his ear hurts. He's not used to women like—" Mrs. Short stopped and pursed her lips. "Well, let's just say, most of the women around here wear sweaters to keep their necks warm. This is Alaska, after all, not Las Vegas. It might be September on the calendar, but we're already feeling the nip of winter. Besides, we're a small, decent town."

Maryann half-expected the fancy women to

be offended, but it was clear they weren't even listening to Mrs. Short. They had all stood by now and were arching their backs and puffing up their hair as they stared at *him*.

Alex stood in the open door of the exam room. The sunlight streamed through the window behind him and made him look bronzed. Maryann blinked. How had that happened? He was wearing the same white lab coat with a stethoscope hanging around his neck that he'd been wearing all day. But he looked different. Maybe because of the angle of the light behind him the lab coat suddenly showed that his shoulders were satisfyingly broad. His dark hair was ruffled and his blue eyes were fringed with black lashes. If it weren't for the look of dawning horror on his clean-shaven face, he could have graced the cover of *GQ* magazine. It would have all been comical if Maryann didn't feel called upon to do something to rescue him.

He cleared his throat and the women looked like they would swoon.

She looked at the salivating women staring at him. So, the man was good-looking. Well, okay, more than good-looking. That didn't mean he was a rock star or anything.

"What's wrong?" Alex finally asked. "Is someone hurt?"

He sounded so suspicious that she had to smile. Maybe he didn't realize how great he looked standing there.

"Careful. They're all—" Maryann started, but she was too late. The women had broken rank and were rushing toward Alex, waving their hands in the air. There was only one thing to do, she decided, as she put her fingers to her lips and gave a shrill referee whistle.

There was a moment of absolute silence. Even Alex looked stunned.

Maryann gave a decisive nod. She had taken a self-defense class in high school and the whistle was all she had mastered, but today it was enough. "First, Mrs. Short, you take Johnny out on the porch. I'll be out in a second to give him his lollipop—he likes lime, doesn't he? We'll set up a follow-up appointment. Everyone else sit back down, except for the doctor, of course."

She was almost surprised when everyone obeyed her.

"These women say they need to see you." Maryann waited for the Shorts to leave the room before raising her eyes to Alex. "For medical reasons."

The doctor nodded and turned to the seated women. He looked stern enough to make

Maryann glad she wasn't one of the fancy women.

"I'm a pediatrician. You'll have to go down the street to Dr. Logan's office. He's the general doctor in town." And then, as though he wasn't sure they understood, Alex added. "I only take children as patients."

"I already told them that—" Maryann started, but she was ignored.

"My feet haven't grown much since I was a girl." Delilah stood up and moved a step closer to Alex, before taking his arm. "And it hurts to walk. Really, feet are feet. It doesn't matter if I'm a child or not. Men always tell me I have such nice-looking ankles."

Delilah stood on her toes so her ankles showed to their best advantage. "What do you think, Doctor?"

Maryann watched the thundercloud settle on Alex's face. He didn't say anything though.

The waif woman sitting in the corner looked up. "Dr. Logan's office is closed this morning." Her voice managed to sound pitiful and sultry at the same time. "There's no place else to go. I need something for all these mosquito bites."

Alex removed Delilah's hands from his arm as he glanced over at the small pink dots on the other woman's arm.

"Baking soda," he said in a curt voice and then looked around. "Just to be sure, are any of you really injured? Or having a heart attack? Even an asthma attack? We'll take an emergency, but that's all. The rest of you will have to see Dr. Logan instead. If he's not there, call later and make an appointment."

The chatter started up. It was impossible to sort out what everyone was saying.

Alex turned and looked at Maryann. "Have them fill out medical forms just in case. And find out if that one woman is allergic to insect bites. Then come back to the exam room. We need to talk."

"Yes, sir." Maryann resisted the impulse to salute. She was in trouble enough as it was. He probably expected she should have locked the door when she saw the women coming.

Alex had no sooner turned to go back to the room when Maryann heard footsteps running up to the porch. She recognized a medical emergency when she heard one and wasn't surprised when Alex turned around to face the door.

"Everybody sit down. Clear some space. We have a patient coming in." Alex said as he headed toward the door. At times like this he blessed the workmen who had made the new doorway and the ramp outside both sturdy and wide.

He'd been through this drill often enough up here, he thought to himself. A siren never announced an emergency as it did back in Los Angeles; here it was the thump of the heavy boots the men wore. The faster the footsteps were coming up the steps to his porch, the worse the problem. The most serious injuries came by the steps and not the ramp; it was in recovery that the patient used a wheelchair. Alex had the door open before the men outside could touch it.

"It's Timmy Fields," the man standing in front said as he pushed his cap back on his forehead and looked behind him to where two other burly men in flannel shirts were carrying the boy. They were all breathing hard and the boy was moaning.

"Easy now," Alex said when he saw how they were carrying his patient. Every spring he gave a first aid emergency course and showed people how to transport injured hikers, but it never seemed like the right people came. Next time he was going to go down to one of the bars and give his demonstration there. Oh—he stopped. He'd be gone by then. He'd have to leave a note for the next doctor. Or maybe Dr. Logan would do it, although people didn't tend to bring him the emergency cases since he lived a mile from town and most problems seemed to happen after the clinics were closed.

"Lay him down here." Alex put his hand on the gurney Maryann had just wheeled over to him.

"Thanks," he said to her as she stepped back so the men would have enough room. Maryann always knew what to do without him telling her.

Together the men gently laid the boy down.

"What happened?" Alex asked the men as his hand reached out to take the boy's pulse. It had been several weeks since he'd seen eight-year-old Timmy for that cough of his. The boy's skin was clammy now, but Alex doubted it was from fever. It was pain making him sweat.

"We found him up on Chilkoot Pass. Fool kid shouldn't have been up there alone. He said some tourists gave him a ride out of town to the base. They should be shot for leaving a kid like that there by himself. Don't know what he was doing. He must have slipped on some rocks or something. We wouldn't have found him if we hadn't been out looking for that Lawson fellow—the one who's been missing."

Alex nodded. He'd been on the search team that had come upon Tucker Lawson's crashed plane. They'd found some blood and his business card with a stake driven through it, but there was no one around. Searchers, under the direction of the sheriff, had been looking for the man, or his remains, since then. Surely the boy hadn't been up there looking for Lawson, though.

Timmy groaned.

"Easy now," Alex said as the boy started to move. "Let me check you out first."

"He's got a lump on his head," one of the men said.

"I see that," Alex said as he ran his fingers over the rest of the boy's scalp, then he turned to Maryann. "Flash—"

"Here."

"Thanks." She'd given him the flashlight before he'd even gotten the word out. Things like this were why he'd promised to write her a letter of recommendation and leave it for the next pediatrician that came here. She was an excellent nurse. She didn't insist on being personal with him, either. His last nurse had wanted him to—well, he wasn't sure what she had wanted. She'd resigned when he refused to have dinner with her one night after work.

Timmy opened one eye and stared.

"Don't worry about focusing," the doctor murmured to the boy before remembering to use simpler words. "Don't worry about what you see. It might be fuzzy."

"I see an angel choir," Timmy said in quiet awe.

Alex choked back his chuckle as he looked over his shoulder. Children were so honest about their feelings. He saw that Maryann was doing the impossible and getting the fancy women to exit the room. All those women with their dyed blonde hair and sparkling gold might look like a band of angels because of the sun shining on their jewelry as they tip-toed past the gurney, especially when Maryann wore her white uniform to usher them out. No wonder Timmy saw angels.

"Don't worry," he said. "It's Nurse Jenner and some friends of hers."

"They're not my friends," Maryann protested from the door as the men who'd carried Timmy down the mountain followed the last of the fancy women out of the clinic. Alex realized with a jolt that he was teasing Maryann. He'd never done that with any of his other nurses. He believed in professionalism in the clinic. But he liked the way her cheeks pinked up and her brown eyes sparked with indignation. She had dark, fringed bangs, and her hair shone as it floated around her head in the breeze from the open door.

"Is she an angel?" the boy asked.

"Some days," Alex said. Then he forgot himself enough to grin at Maryann. He decided it would be okay to relax with her; he'd be gone before long, so what could it hurt?

Maryann tried to give him a stern look, but the blush on her face spoiled the effect. She shut the open door, but her hair still floated around her face.

"Does that mean I'm dead?" Timmy asked with some anticipation.

Alex looked down at the boy and smiled. "Not today you're not."

"Oh," Timmy said, and with that, he closed his eyes.

Alex looked up at Maryann again, but she was one step ahead of him. She held out an ice pack she'd brought from the back room along with the gurney. He pressed that against Timmy's face. "The cold will wake him up."

"I'll call his parents," Maryann said.

"No." Timmy opened his eyes in alarm. "You can't call them."

"You know we have to," Alex said gently as

he finished running his hands over the boy's legs. "You took quite a fall. Does your leg hurt?"

Timmy winced and nodded. "They'll kill me for sure."

"I'll tell them you're a brave soldier," Maryann said as she walked over to the phone.

Alex imagined she would say those very words to them, too. No one could accuse her of not caring about everyone who stumbled across her path. She was generous to a fault and that was the only reason he could think of for her to have sat in the diner last night talking with her cousin about matching him up with someone. Not that either one of the women had shown an overabundance of caring when Maryann had called him The Ice Man. Wait until that nickname made the rounds of Treasure Creek. He wasn't the kind of person who talked about himself to everyone he met, but he'd helped enough children in this town to have some friends among the parents. He'd been warned about last night's conversation by two sources already.

He watched Maryann as she held the phone to her ear and talked to Timmy's parents. He couldn't hear the words she was saying, but he could hear the soft tones of her voice.

He supposed the matchmaking had been

inevitable. Maryann was the kind of woman who'd bring home stray cats. He knew that when he hired her, but he'd had no other choice. Women like her just couldn't accept that some men—like some animals—were better off alone. She must have sensed the sadness in him and decided marriage was the solution.

He'd meant to tell her today that he was fine with the single life, but he hadn't quite figured out the right words. Usually, he'd just blurt it out. He didn't know why he was hesitating. As near as he could figure, he didn't want to make her feel bad for caring that he was alone. Also, it bothered him that she thought of him as an ice man, and part of him wanted to prove her wrong.

He must be going soft from living in Treasure Creek. People around here wanted to be connected. They weren't content with just loving their neighbor, they wanted to know where the guy was going for Sunday dinner, and if he needed help defrosting anything. Maybe it was some primitive emotional throwback to the freezing winters of old when people relied on their tribes for a safe existence. People needed other people then. And at least in this small town, that feeling seemed to still hold true.

He hadn't thought much about that until one day when people came from miles around for a simple funeral. Even if people didn't know the old man who'd died, they knew someone who knew someone who knew him. So they mourned the loss of those connections. The tribe had been lessened.

And then every year there was a Christmas pageant at the church that attracted the whole community. Even though he hadn't been going to church, he'd always been drawn to the pageant.

He wasn't used to a place like this. He envied the people here their connections, but he didn't belong.

He should head south for Los Angeles as soon as he could. He'd been saving his money for years so he could open a clinic there. No one would be inviting him to any Christmas pageant down in L.A.

Not that he had time to think about that now, when it looked like Timmy had a fractured bone in his leg as well as the bump on his head. What had the boy been doing out on the pass, anyway?

Maryann hung up the phone and turned back to them. Alex could see why Timmy had been confused enough to think she was some celestial being. Her pink cheeks made her glow. She looked sweet. He had a hard time believing she had talked so openly about his personal life in front of everyone. If she knew anything about the tour guides of Treasure Creek, she'd know they would be making jokes at his expense from now until he left here. In fact, they'd be making jokes about it long after he was gone.

But seeing her in front of him, he couldn't convince himself she'd meant any harm. Maybe the gossips had it wrong and it had been her cousin who had said those things about him. That thought made him feel better, although he didn't dare ask himself why he cared which woman had spoken what.

Chapter Two

Maryann put another cool cloth on Timmy's head. His breathing was still ragged, and Alex had given him a shot to help with the pain in his leg. Alex planned to put a splint on the injured limb as soon as the boy's parents came, so he'd gone into the back room to pick out what he needed from the supply cabinet. Ordinarily, Maryann would have done that, but Timmy had asked her to stay with him and Alex had nodded his agreement.

"You've got to pray for me," Timmy whispered to Maryann as soon as Alex left the room. He was still lying on the gurney and she had pulled a sheet over his legs. "Times are dire."

"Dire?" She was surprised he even knew the word at his age.

But he nodded. "Bad. Real bad."

"You know I'm not really an angel, don't you?" She reached under the gurney to find another pillow. "I can pray for you, but I have no special powers."

Timmy nodded. "It's just for when my parents come in. Look like you're praying for me. And do you have a Bible? They never yell when there's a Bible around."

She stopped, the pillow still in her hands, to look at the boy. "Your parents don't hit you, do they?"

She'd only seen the Fields in passing. They must be Christians, if Timmy wanted a Bible. On the other hand, she knew some people took the Bible and twisted what it had to say. She had no idea why Timmy would be so intent on reminding his parents of their faith, unless he was afraid of them.

"They yell a lot," Timmy admitted. "And my mom cries some."

"But do they hit you?"

Timmy shook his head. "You're still going to pray though, aren't you?"

"I'll see what I can do." Maryann set the pillow on the end of the gurney where Timmy's legs didn't reach. Then she walked over to the drawer where she kept her belongings. She carried a small Bible with her. She'd been going to the church here with her cousin, and

re-connecting with her childhood faith. It had
been a long time since she had regularly read
a Bible like she was doing nowadays. Her tur-
bulent adolescence, as she played referee to
her parents' arguments and subsequent new
loves, had caused her to drift far away from
God, like it was His fault in some way that
she had to endure it. She was glad to be back.
Her restored belief centered her; she should
have never stopped going to church and praying. Even those bad years would have been
better.

She held the white Bible up for Timmy to
see. "You can borrow this if you want to read
something."

"Put it in my hands like I'm dead." Timmy
crossed his arms over his chest and closed his
eyes.

"I most certainly will not." Maryann walked
back to the gurney with the book in her hand.
"Your parents are worried enough as it is."
Then she thought a moment. "Besides, it's
a girl's Bible. You'd look too sweet in your
casket if you were holding it. You could as
well be holding a bouquet of lilies."

"Oh." Timmy opened his eyes and frowned
at the Bible. "I don't want to hold no girl's
Bible."

"I didn't think so," Maryann said as she

laid the Bible beside him. "But it won't hurt to have it close, just in case. Like you're alive and reading it. You might try a psalm."

"Maybe you could put a ninja sticker on it." Timmy cautiously took hold of the Bible. "Then it'd be okay for boys."

Maryann smiled.

She heard more footsteps on the porch and turned to the door. "I bet that's your parents."

Maryann walked over to greet the Fields as they opened the door and stepped inside.

"Where is he?" Mrs. Fields asked breathlessly, even as her eyes came to rest on the gurney. She was a slight woman with a harried expression on her face, and she was wearing a stained sweatshirt. Maryann remembered that there were a couple of children younger than Timmy in the family. They were all due for shots and Alex had them on the list for her to call.

"What kind of a fool thing were you doing, boy?" Mr. Fields asked as he followed his wife into the room. He was overweight and puffing hard, but he zeroed in on Timmy right away. "You know better than taking off like that."

Maryann saw Timmy's face crumple in misery.

She stepped back to the gurney. "I was just going to say a prayer for Timmy. Would you both join me?"

"Oh." Mrs. Fields looked up in surprise.

"I—" Mr. Fields started to say something, then stopped.

Maryann walked closer to Timmy and winked at him. She had a moment's hesitation. It had been a long time since she'd prayed in public and she wasn't sure if it was the right thing for her to do now since it was all for show. Of course, it was for Timmy's benefit and God loved children, so it would likely be all right with Him. She bowed her head and started.

"God of all the beings on earth and in heaven," she began. She thought Timmy would like that since he seemed preoccupied with death and angels. "Timmy here is hurting, and we ask that you make him comfortable. He feels bad for what he did and he asks You to help him do better next time. Amen."

"Amen," the Fields both muttered.

When Maryann opened her eyes, she saw that Timmy had been right. His parents did look subdued. They moved over to their son and each gave him a pat on his head before moving back and looking at Maryann, as though waiting for further direction. She nodded approvingly at them, and smoothed the sheets on the gurney. She heard them walk away from the gurney and stop by the door.

They had started talking to each other, thinking she couldn't hear them. If everything else hadn't been so quiet, they would have been right, she admitted to herself.

"You were supposed to be watching him," Mr. Fields hissed at his wife.

"Me? You should have been watching him," Mrs. Fields said, her voice low and tense. "It's not like you're working anymore. You should at least help with the kids."

"It's not my fault I can't find work. These are hard times and you know it. Besides, you're his mother. Don't lay it all on me."

Maryann looked down at Timmy. He could hear his parents, too, and embarrassment covered his face. She remembered what it felt like when her parents were arguing. If someone outside her family heard them, she'd wanted to disappear.

"The doctor will be here in a minute," Maryann said in her most professional voice. Maybe the couple wouldn't know she had heard them. If she was calm enough, she might even fool Timmy. "In fact, I think I hear him now."

The voices all stopped. And then, as if on cue, Alex walked into the room.

Something inside her applauded. He might be an ice man, but she could count on him to show up when she needed him.

"Doctor," Mrs. Fields said, looking up and giving him a tight smile, "how is he?"

"Your son will be fine. He's running a slight fever. Keep him inside and warm. Let me know if he develops a cough or the fever goes higher. But the immediate thing is that he fractured a bone in his right leg. I'm setting up a splint for it now. I just want your signature before I treat him."

"Can it wait?" Mr. Fields asked with a forced smile on his face. "Don't bones sometimes heal by themselves?"

"Wait?" Alex looked taken aback. "I'm afraid not in this case."

Mrs. Fields stepped closer. "How much will it be, doctor?" She kept shifting the handle on her purse from one side to the other. "I get paid next week, but—"

"We'll pay our bill somehow," Mr. Fields finished for her. His face was red with embarrassment. "We might need to wait until our Permanent Fund checks come. I lost my job. It was the one that carried our health insurance, but we'll get you paid somehow—" He looked at Alex. "You've been here long enough to know about the Permanent Fund checks? They're the ones we get from the state for all the oil that's pumped out of Alaska? Those checks are good as gold."

"Ah." Alex cleared his throat. "Sure, I know about the checks. Don't worry, though. I don't have the figures added up, but I could use some new shelves in the waiting room. If you're interested, we could trade services." He looked at Mr. Fields. "I hear you're a good carpenter."

"I've nailed a few boards together in my time," Mr. Fields said proudly. "Your shelves are as good as done. I can come back later today to measure everything."

Alex nodded. "Good. I have some lumber in the back we can use."

"Thank you," Mrs. Fields muttered.

Maryann watched the whole scene with satisfaction. She knew she was right that the children of Treasure Creek needed this doctor. She only had to look at the sudden hero worship in Timmy's eyes to know that. Alex didn't make anyone look small, and that won him the respect of his young patients.

"We'll just take Timmy in the back and get him set up," Alex said as he motioned for Maryann to follow him. He looked at Mrs.

Fields. "I'll need to cut the leg off his jeans, but I'll do it as carefully as I can, so you can sew them back together later."

The woman nodded. "Thanks. He doesn't have enough pairs as it is."

"Say, Doc," Mr. Fields said from beside the door. "If the shelves aren't enough, my wife here can introduce you to some of the local women. You know, it'd be like one of those matchmaking services they have in the big cities."

"What?" Alex turned to look at the man.

"I heard you were looking," Mr. Fields said as he reached for the doorknob. "We could help you out. Nothing fancy, but the wife here knows everyone. She'll fix you up."

Maryann felt the breath leave her body. She had a bad feeling about this.

"Hush about that." Mrs. Fields turned to her husband. "How can you be thinking about that when our son lies there in pain?"

Then the woman turned to the doctor. "Should we go back in the room with you when you work on Timmy's leg?"

Maryann risked glancing at Alex. His face looked frozen.

"I'm fine." Timmy spoke up from where he lay.

Maryann noticed the boy had a strong grip

on that small Bible of hers. She wished she was the one holding it, though.

"Maybe you and Dad could wait here," Timmy added. It looked as if there was a ragged piece of old paper peeking out from the pages of the Bible. Timmy must have put it there. "In this room."

"Well, I guess." Mrs. Fields muttered, as if she didn't know what to do.

"I could wait with you if you'd like," Maryann offered. The doctor didn't really need her for the splint. Besides, she'd give anything not to have to face him right now. She could tell he knew all about the conversation she and her cousin had had about him. "We have a few magazines on the table by the chairs."

She saw Timmy's parents sit down in two chairs and noted they left an empty one between them. She figured that was where Timmy usually sat. No wonder the boy was torn apart by their arguing; he'd grown up right in the middle of things. Just as she had.

"Nurse Jenner. You're with me," Alex said before she even moved.

"Yes," she said as she gave the chairs one last look and walked toward the gurney.

"Here, I can do that." Alex reached the gurney first and put his hands on it.

"But I usually push the patients. That's my job."

"We're a team," Alex said, wheeling the gurney back to the examining room.

Well, Maryann thought, *what was that supposed to mean?* If she didn't know better, she'd think The Ice Man was melting. But that was unlikely. Perhaps he was planning to fire her. Not that she could blame him if he did. She hadn't intended for the whole town to be talking about Alex's love life. When would she ever learn to keep her mouth shut?

"It was a mistake," Maryann muttered, as she followed Alex down the hall. "That conversation with my cousin."

Alex finished pushing the gurney into the room and Maryann turned on the lights.

"We can talk about that later, Nurse Jenner," he said.

Maryann nodded as she stepped closer to the gurney and bent slightly to adjust a corner of the sheet. At least Alex wouldn't fire her as long as there was a patient around to hear him do it.

Timmy gave a weak snicker.

"What?" She glanced over at the boy. His face was still pale, but his eyes were mischievous.

"You still look like an angel," he said, and chuckled a little louder.

Maryann straightened up and glanced at the mirror by the sink. Her hair was just as windblown as it had been after she'd stepped outside to give Johnny Short that lime lollipop. Why did her hair always have to look so wild? It was puffed up in a circle around her head. No wonder Alex hadn't shown any interest in the women up here. He probably liked women with their hair smoothly drawn back in elegant styles, like the models wore in those glossy magazines. Ever since last night, she'd wondered what kind of a woman he would marry. She hadn't meant to accept her cousin's challenge, but she'd been thinking about it ever since.

She eyed Alex as he stood beside the gurney. Whoever he married would need to fit into the world of a prosperous doctor in Los Angeles. Those fancy women were probably right about the expensive cars he would drive. Cooperative hair would be important. He'd want a young trophy wife to ride in his red BMW convertible. Or maybe it would be a top of the line Lexus.

"You might want an angel by your side for the next few minutes," Alex muttered to the boy, as he removed the sheet that had covered his leg. "I'll have to cut off part of your jeans before we can set your leg."

Timmy nodded.

"It'll do my best to be careful, but it's bound to hurt some." Alex smoothed down the sheet beside the boy.

"Okay," Timmy said, as he gripped the Bible.

"I can take that for you," Alex said, as he held out his hand for the book.

Maryann noticed the boy was reluctant to give it up. "We can put it on the shelf by the doctor's desk," she said. "You'll be able to see it."

Timmy shook his head.

Alex looked over at her. "It's okay. He can keep it."

It was time for them to get to work.

Alex was focused on getting the plaster splint on Timmy's leg quickly. At times like these, he liked working with an efficient nurse like Maryann. Even though he could sense she was nervous, she anticipated what instruments he'd need and she had them ready for him. More importantly, she kept up a steady stream of soft conversation with the patient, so he didn't need to think of words to say to distract the patient. For some reason, she was talking about cars today.

He'd given a local anesthetic to Timmy to dull most of the pain in his leg, and the boy was groggy, but Timmy still laughed at Maryann's chatter.

"There. We're done," Alex said, as he finished the splint.

"I think our patient will need a minute to recover," Maryann said.

He looked up at Timmy's face and saw he was almost asleep. The book had slipped from his hands and was lying on the gurney beside him.

Alex picked up the Bible. "I'll move this to the shelf so it won't fall off the gurney."

"Careful with it," Maryann said.

Alex nodded as he walked over to the bookcase. "Timmy sure is attached to it. Although I suppose that's true for lots of children."

"It's natural for children to believe in God," Maryann said, with a nod.

Alex grunted as he laid the Bible down on an empty shelf. "Maybe, but it passes soon enough."

Maryann looked over at him curiously. "Why do you say that?"

"The minute we're born people start having problems. Sooner or later, everyone comes up with a problem God can't solve for them. And it's usually sooner."

"Oh." Maryann looked at him and then blinked.

"I'm not the only one who has been disappointed in God," he added, softly. The sympathy in her brown eyes grew and he found the words escaping him. "And, at that, I'm better off than—" He broke off, but he didn't stop. "Well, I'm better off than my brother."

Alex held his breath. He never talked about God or his brother. He must be more bothered than he'd thought about Maryann calling him The Ice Man. Why did women judge a man by how easily he spilled his emotions, anyway? Or maybe it had nothing to do with her. Maybe it was the confidence Timmy had in his face when he held onto that Bible. It made Alex remember the way he used to feel a long time ago. Back then, he'd embraced God in the same way he loved his pet frog and the stack of comics under his bed. It was all part of a carefree childhood.

But then came the moment when everything that was good in his family shattered— the day Alex's life had been spared when his older brother shoved him out of the way of a runaway car. Even though they had carefully checked that the light in front of them said it was okay to walk, the car's brakes had failed and the driver couldn't stop for the two boys crossing the road. Within seconds, Alex had landed safely back on the sidewalk, while his brother, Frank Rocco Havens, was crumpled on the street, with his body so damaged he'd never walk again.

"You mean your brother that phones?" Maryann finally asked.

Alex nodded. "His first name is Frank, but we don't call him that anymore."

Now, why did he have to say that? He never even thought about Rocco's old name anymore. Their mother was the one who had renamed Frank after the accident. The first time she'd heard another kid draw the name Frank out into Frankenstein, she'd told the family they'd use Frank's middle name, Rocco, from now on. His mother had been kind back in those early days; she fought the whole system to get her son care. It wasn't until later, when the doctors said his brother would always be paralyzed, that she drew away from the rest of the family. Shortly after that his father started traveling more.

Alex had felt like it had been only him and Rocco that made up the family after that. Alex had to fight his guilt, wondering why he couldn't have stayed out of the crosswalk that day, instead of trailing behind his brother who'd already made it clear he wasn't to come with him. If Rocco had been alone when the car came, he could have jumped to safety. Instead, he'd turned and pushed Alex out of the way. Alex had idolized his older brother. Couldn't he have obeyed and stayed behind just that once?

"I'm sorry," he finally said. He looked over at Maryann. "I don't mean to stand here talking about someone you don't even know."

"But I feel like I do know Rocco a little," Maryann answered gently. "I didn't know his real name was Frank, but when he calls, I answer the phone. He always wants to know what the weather is like up here, so I look out the window and describe what I see. Once we saw a bald eagle fly by."

Alex was surprised. "I thought he just asked to speak to me and that you put him straight through. He doesn't usually talk to strangers."

"I'm not a stranger, I'm your nurse," Maryann said. "Besides, he seems nice. He likes what I say about the mountains. Why wouldn't he talk to people?"

Alex could hardly say it was because Rocco was bitter. His brother's mouth might still work, but he was so self-conscious about his legs he'd managed to become a recluse in the middle of the largest city on the west coast.

Granted, Rocco hadn't sounded as grim the last few times Alex had talked to him, but something was wrong. Rocco kept saying he wanted to talk in person and Alex kept saying he needed to just speak on the phone for now. Alex would be in Los Angeles in three weeks anyway, so he couldn't make a special trip down there now, not when he had so much to do to wrap up his practice here.

"How long does he talk to you anyway?" Alex finally asked.

Maryann shrugged. "It's only a few minutes. He usually wants to know if we have snow on the mountain yet. And what the lunch special is at Lizbet's Diner. And if you've been out on any tours lately as the guide. He's very interested in Treasure Creek. You should invite him up to visit."

"Rocco? He never goes anywhere." Alex's voice sounded harsh to his own ears. He knew Rocco *could* go places, but he never even went to the grocery store anymore.

It was silent again, but finally Maryann said, "Maybe he likes to stay home."

Alex grunted. "He has a choice. I'm not saying it would be easy. He's in a wheelchair. My brother can only go out if someone is with him. I got him an attendant last year, to help him with this exercise program that could make him more independent, and if he wanted to go outside he could—"

Timmy moaned and Alex looked down at the boy.

After that, he and Maryann worked in silence.

By the time they had Timmy ready to go back to the waiting room, the child was almost able to sit up. The boy was still disoriented, but his parents could take him home with crutches.

This time Maryann wheeled the gurney back into the waiting room. Alex swore he could hear her singing a lullaby to the boy as they went down the hall, but he had to get the prescription written, so he sat at his desk in the examination room while she took Timmy back to his parents.

Alex decided it was a good thing he was leaving in a few weeks. This whole thing about the ice man label and people worrying about him getting married had him feeling strange inside. He'd never told anyone about his brother. He didn't know why he was opening his mouth about it now. Fortunately, he'd stopped before he told Maryann everything. Knowing her, she'd just feel sorry for him. Then he'd need to do more than stop her matchmaking, he'd also have to stop her from poking around in his heart to see what his guilt and sadness was all about. And then she'd move on to worrying about Rocco. He knew her kind. And his older brother wasn't any more free with his emotions than Alex was. They'd never even talked about "that day" with each other. There were just no words for some things. Alex wasn't even able to say he was sorry, not until he could do something to make up for the part he'd played in the accident.

When he finished writing the prescription, Alex took it out to where the Fieldses were sitting. He reminded them to bring Timmy back if he developed a cough or high fever, and they agreed. Then they left.

The second the door closed behind the family, Maryann turned to him. "I'm sorry. I had no business saying anything about you last night."

Alex felt himself relax. As long as she forgot about him and Rocco, he didn't care what she wanted to discuss.

"Just for the record," Alex said to keep her talking, "what exactly did you say, anyway?"

He wondered if what he'd heard was true. Maybe she'd said something completely different, and the gossip had turned it into something else.

Maryann hesitated. Her whole face looked pinched by nervousness. "I said that you needed to be poleaxed by love."

"What?" Alex was amazed. "I don't even know what 'poleaxed by love' means."

"It's a Jenner family expression," Maryann muttered. "You get sick. You want to die. All for the sake of love."

"Sounds awful." Alex noticed that his nurse was getting her color back. He felt they had averted some crisis.

Maryann smiled up at him. "I think it is actually. You should see my parents when they're in love. Not with each other, of course. They've been divorced for years. But each time one of them is poleaxed, they stare into the eyes of their latest and get all disoriented just talking about it. They're like children."

Alex was quiet for a bit. Maybe there had been no discontent in the words she'd spoken about him to her cousin after all. "And how about you? Did you ever fall in love like that?"

"Me?" Maryann squeaked. She looked alarmed. And then much too pale. Finally, she shook her head. "I'm immune to that kind of stuff. I've seen it go wrong too many times."

Alex frowned. That didn't seem right. "But surely you plan to get married."

"If I do, I plan to pick my husband based on reason. And genetics. I think good genes are important, don't you?" Her cheeks were still pink, but he suspected it was indignation turning them rosy this time.

"Yes, but…" Alex was taken aback. He'd never met a woman who didn't long to feel some intense emotions, especially when it came to marriage. He knew he had a reputation for being a little detached, but it didn't seem right for someone like Maryann to feel that way, too.

Finally her face went back to its normal color, and she swallowed. "Look. There's no need to beat around the bush about what happened the other night. I want you to know I didn't mean anything by it. I was just talking with my cousin about how much I wanted you to stay on as the doctor here and, before you know it, she was talking about how you'd stay if you met someone to marry."

Alex was beginning to feel better already. "So she was the one who was supposed to match me up with someone?"

Maryann swallowed again. "No, that was me."

"You're the one who was supposed to help

me get poleaxed? With some woman you picked out?" He wondered if Maryann knew how cute she was. Funny, he'd never noticed before how her nose turned up just enough to make her look mischievous. And her eyes—the gold flecks in the brown made them look like they were twinkling. "I suppose I should be grateful I have a strong constitution. That whole thing sounds a bit tough."

"Now see, that's why I told my cousin I shouldn't mention anything to you. I knew you'd just make fun of it and—"

Alex put up his hand. "I think it's kind of sweet that you're worried."

The sun was shining in the window and Maryann's face lit up in a smile. "You do?"

"You're not thinking of one of those fancy women, I hope." Alex said, wondering why he was going so easy on her.

Maryann shook her head. "I was thinking of Belinda Edwards."

"Who?" Alex's smile disappeared. He hadn't really thought she had someone specific in mind for him. That changed everything.

Maryann took a step back. "You know. She's the single mom who works in the office at the grade school. Long red hair and glasses. Midtwenties. She's taking some online college courses to improve herself. She likes camping and watching DVDs at home. I'm pretty sure she'd go out with you if you asked."

Alex was stunned. He still couldn't believe it. "You haven't just been talking? You've actually been matching me up?"

"Well, I haven't asked her if she's interested, but she does seem nice."

Suddenly Alex didn't feel like teasing her anymore. How could she call him an ice man, when she was trying to marry him off to someone he'd never even had a conversation with? That was more than a little cold. "Do you even know this woman?"

"Belinda gets her hair cut at the same place I do. She's got gorgeous hair, by the way. And I like her."

"You haven't been in Treasure Creek much more than a month. How often have you had your hair cut in that time?" he asked.

Alex couldn't believe Maryann was standing there smiling at him, like he should be grateful she was trying to find some woman to marry him. Like he was desperate. Like he didn't have things he needed to do before he settled down and got married.

"I don't have time to date anyone," Alex said with as much dignity as he could manage. "Now, if you'll excuse me, I need to do some paperwork."

He walked down to the exam room and closed the door. He didn't have anything to write, and she probably knew it.

But at least he'd gotten away with his self-respect intact. He'd been so sure the story had been reported to him with errors. He hadn't admitted it to himself until now, but he'd been confident she'd started that conversation with her cousin because Maryann was interested in dating him herself. *Her,* not some Belinda Edwards who liked to camp.

He had been planning to turn Maryann down gently, of course. They'd had a quiet friendship that was building during the time she'd been here, and he was afraid to disrupt that. He didn't want her to hand in her resignation as his previous nurse had done, either. But apparently he'd been mistaken. She wasn't interested in dating him at all.

It took him a moment or two, but he finally told himself it was for the best.

He already had his plane tickets to leave in three weeks. He'd get someone to fly him to Juneau, and then on to Anchorage. He'd take a flight south from there. A month from now, he'd be looking for property in Los Angeles where he'd build his clinic.

He had plans. He'd been awarded a large grant from a local foundation to cover the cost of the ground he needed. And he'd saved every extra penny he made moonlighting as a tour guide up here, to help with the construction. He'd have to take out a loan of course, but his savings would provide just enough for the needed downpayment. Until he did something to pay back his brother for saving his life, Alex didn't feel free to live a normal life. The small clinic would be named after his brother.

After all, Rocco couldn't get married, since he couldn't even meet a woman, as long as he confined himself to their parents' house. Worse yet, his brother couldn't realize his childhood hope of being a surgeon, not with his hands and his legs as crippled as they were by the accident. Alex knew he could never give his brother his dreams back, but the plaque for the clinic he planned to build would show his brother how much he appreciated the sacrifice he had made.

He needed to do *something* before he could even say he was sorry.

He'd tried to give his brother other things in the past. So far, the only thing Rocco had accepted was the money to pay for that attendant. His brother said no to anything else, saying money couldn't buy him what he really needed. There was nothing else Alex could give him, except a clinic built in his name. He knew Rocco liked the idea, because he smiled every time Alex mentioned it. Maybe, once the clinic was built, Rocco's bitterness would fade.

And if Rocco was happier, maybe Alex could ask him for forgiveness. Maybe his parents could also forgive the past and live in the present. Right now, no one was free of the accident. His parents avoided each other and Rocco. Maybe, when the clinic was completed and Alex was home, he'd have his family back again.

Chapter Three

Later that afternoon, Maryann was sitting at a small desk in the waiting room, staring at the wall when the bell over the door rang. She should have been going through the list of patients to call for tomorrow's appointments, but she'd become distracted thinking about what had happened that morning. Alex was in the examining room and it was good that he was. She felt closer to him because of what he'd told her about his brother, and farther apart at the same time, because of the gossip she'd caused. Mostly, she didn't want to think about it, even though she couldn't get it out of her head.

"Amy!" Maryann said as she looked up and saw the owner of the local tour company. The young red-haired widow always had a smile on her face, and she was one of Maryann's favorite people in Treasure Creek.

For the first time, it occurred to her that Amy James came to the office more than was necessary. There always seemed to be a good reason about the twins to stop by, but maybe she was interested in Alex in a romantic way. Maryann wondered if the answer to who the doctor should marry was right in front of her.

"Here to see the doctor?" Maryann asked, keeping her voice neutral. She should feel more excitement at the thought that she might be talking to Alex's future wife, especially because Amy had deep roots in this place and could convince Alex to stay.

Oh—Maryann just remembered that she hadn't combed her hair back into place after being out in the wind.

"Am I interrupting something?" Amy walked over to the desk. "I can come back."

Amy was always neatly dressed, and Maryann didn't want to look like a hooligan. Not that she was competing with Amy for anyone's attention. It was just that all women liked to look their best.

Maryann smiled. "No, I just—well, my hair." Then she reached up to smooth her hair back into its usual bobbed shape.

Amy laughed a little. "That happens up here, especially this time of year. I know it's happened to me. Of course, Ben always thought it was funny. I'd be there with my hair going every which way, and he'd be grinning like a kid at the circus."

The widow's laugh faded as she remembered her late husband. Then she seemed to shake off her memories. "Well, I just came around because I'm putting together a choir for the Christmas pageant, and I wondered if you'd come help us sing."

"Oh, I can't," Maryann said as she heard footsteps in the hall. "I'm not much of a singer."

Amy shrugged. "That's not important. Ben always said it was the spirit of the thing that counted. I'm hoping to do the best pageant ever, in his honor this year, but I'm not sure I'm up to it. I figure if we can get started early by practicing the carols, we'll have a chance of pulling it off."

Alex entered the room. "The pageant is nice. Every year it gets a little better."

"Well, that's going to be hard to do this year," Amy said, as she sat down in one of the waiting room chairs. "I'm hoping that, if we can get going now, maybe we'll gain some enthusiasm."

"Well, I'm sure whatever you do will be great," Alex said, then he looked at the woman more closely. "Are you all right?"

Maryann watched Alex walk over to Amy. Now why did he have to stand there and look at the woman as if she was a delicate flower?

"I can give you a vitamin B shot if you need one," Alex offered as he reached out his hand to touch Amy's forehead. "You've been going through a tough time. If anything troubles you, let me know."

Maryann hoped none of the fancy women heard about Alex being willing to treat Amy, even though she wasn't a child.

Amy looked up at him and Maryann wondered if the two of them needed to be alone.

"I have been worried," the widow said softly before Maryann could think of an excuse to leave. "Something's been missing and I don't know where…well, it's the treasure map we talked about. You know the one?"

Then Amy dropped her voice even further, until Maryann couldn't hear her words. Maryann walked toward her desk and sat down to finish the filing she had to do. She told herself she should be happy. She wanted Alex to stay in Treasure Creek. If he fell in love with Amy, he'd have to stay. Maybe the treasure map that Amy's sons had found would bring them together. Some people thought the map showed where an ancestor of Amy's had hidden the gold.

Maryann saw Alex frown as he looked down at Amy. "That doesn't sound good. Have you reported that it's gone?"

Maryann couldn't help but notice that he didn't act anything like The Ice Man when talking to Amy. He leaned over her most solicitously. Maybe it was only nurses and fancy women Alex wanted to avoid. She supposed he figured one was work and the others were gold diggers.

"I don't want to report it to anyone official yet," Amy said in a louder voice and gave a glance at Maryann. Then she shook her head and turned back to Alex. "I just wanted to ask you to keep your eyes open."

Alex nodded.

"Anyway," Amy said with a bright smile that included Maryann, "I hope you can both sing in the pageant."

"I'll pass," Alex said as he turned to go into the exam room.

Maryann tried to remind herself of her goal to get Alex to stay in town.

"You should sing," Maryann said.

Alex frowned. "What's the point? I'm not going to be in town for the pageant."

"Well, coming to a few practices wouldn't hurt," Maryann said. "Maybe some other men will join if they see you're practicing."

Alex lifted an eyebrow in protest. "I'm not that influential."

"You are," Amy stepped in, fairly gushing. "And it's not just the men you'll inspire. I'm sure half of the single women in town will volunteer, too, if you do. That'll give me plenty of people for the choir."

Maryann figured Amy had underestimated the doctor's impact. If all of the single women were there, the single men wouldn't be far behind.

"You won't need to wear a costume or anything," Amy promised.

"But," Alex tried again, "You need to remember I won't be here at Christmas. I'll be down in Los Angeles, putting together my new clinic."

"Oh," Amy said. "That's right."

Maryann felt her enthusiasm fall to the floor right along with Amy's. He was still so set on leaving town.

"You could still practice with us," Amy finally said. "Even just one or two times might be enough to get the women there.

You wouldn't even need to sing. Just stand around. I could put you in charge of lighting or something."

"I could do that," Alex said. "I'm sorry I won't be here for the pageant."

"Thanks," Amy said, and then straightened up as if she was bracing herself. "I was going to wait a few weeks to start rehearsals, but I better get them going now."

"Three weeks," Alex reminded her. "That's how long I'll be here." Then he grinned. "Maryann will be there, too. She can take over my place when I'm gone. Singing."

"But I—" she sputtered.

"That's perfect," Amy beamed at them both and stood. "I better get going so I can tell everyone. We have the tour team meeting tonight so we'll plan to meet Thursday night at the church for the carol rehearsal. Let's say five-thirty to nine."

"People can't sing for three and a half hours," Maryann managed to gasp. "Not amateurs anyway."

"You're right," Amy said. "We'll need snacks and something to drink. Maybe hot tea. We'll take a nice long break."

"They'll still strain their vocal chords," Maryann added.

"That's it." Amy snapped her fingers and

looked at Alex. "You can be the choir doctor. You won't have to sing a note."

"I treat children," Alex protested.

"That's why you're perfect," Amy said as she headed for the door. "Children are screaming all the time."

Maryann and Alex both watched her walk toward the door. Just before she got there, Amy turned around. "Oh, and Maryann, why don't you come to our team meeting with Alex tonight? I've wanted to get your perspective on our tours, since you're new in the area. You know, specialty tours, that sort of thing."

"But I—" Maryann protested.

"It won't take long," Amy assured her as she turned the knob and half-opened the door. "We're meeting for hamburgers in the back room at Lizbet's Diner at seven." And then Amy turned to flash a smile at Maryann. "I hear you like eating there."

With that, the other woman turned to walk through the door.

"She knows," Maryann muttered glumly as the door was closed.

"The whole town knows," Alex replied.

They stood there for a minute.

Finally, he put his hands in his pockets.

"I have those insurance forms to fill out, so I plan to stay late tonight. I'll just walk over to Lizbet's at seven, if you want to go with me."

Maryann nodded. "I have some paperwork, too." She paused. "You know, I'm really sorry I said anything last night."

"Well, what's done is done," he said briskly. "In the meantime, we have a clinic to run."

Alex walked back to the desk in his exam room and opened the bottom drawer. He'd sent away for the plaque a month ago, and it had only arrived last week. He liked rubbing his hands over the engraved brass plate. "The Frank Rocco Havens Clinic," it read.

Just holding the plaque made him feel good. His plans for the clinic were the reason he moonlighted with Amy's tour company. Every Saturday during tourist season, he'd taken a busload of people up along the Klondike Highway. He knew more about the gold rush that had ignited Alaska in the late 1800s than the men who had lived through it had probably known. He was certainly making more money off it than most of them had.

He wondered why Amy wanted him and Maryann at tonight's meeting. He didn't always attend the meetings, because he was part time, and, as far as he knew, Amy had never asked any outsider to come and give their feedback on the tours. Not that it was a bad idea, he told himself. She just hadn't done it before.

He looked at the clock on his desk. He had things to do, so he spent fifteen minutes writing up some notes from this morning.

"Doctor?"

Alex looked up to see Maryann standing in the open doorway.

"Sally Weston is here with her mother."

"Send them in," Alex said as he reached down to put the plaque back in the drawer.

His nurse gave him a completely impersonal smile and turned to leave the room. Which annoyed him, even though that is what he wanted her to do.

Maryann walked back to the waiting room.

"The doctor will see you now," Maryann said as she smiled at five-year-old Sally and her mother. "Just go on back."

Maryann waited for the two of them to leave the waiting room before she turned to address Belinda Edwards. By now she should have realized the conversation in the diner last night would have been relayed to Belinda.

Maryann decided she would never talk about anyone's dating life ever again.

Belinda was sitting in one of the padded chairs that lined the right-hand wall of the office. Her red hair was piled on top of her head and anchored with a big clip. Maybe it was because of the red hair, but Maryann couldn't help but compare Belinda to Amy. The woman sitting in the doctor's office now was a lot more casual than the one who'd just left. And Alex didn't strike her as the informal kind.

"So, what'd he say?" Belinda actually snapped her gum.

"I can't ask him on a date for you," Maryann said. "I told you that. I mentioned your name last night, but I spoke too soon. He's not the easiest man to pin down. He says he's got things to do."

"Oh." Belinda stopped chewing and frowned a little. "Well, I'm not going to be around forever. If he wants to date me, he needs to make a move."

"I'm sure he's aware of that," Maryann said. "Maybe you could sign up to sing in the Christmas pageant. You could get to know him there. I hear he's going to be at the first few rehearsals."

"So will all the other women in town. Have you seen those fancy women?"

"Yes, but I'm sure none of them have a beautiful voice like yours," Maryann said soothingly.

Belinda looked up at her in astonishment. "I didn't know you'd heard me sing."

"And you have such beautiful eyes," Maryann finished. She'd heard Belinda humming one day at the beauty salon, and had been impressed. She figured anyone who could hum like that could sing. "Plus, your hair is so shiny. And with your kids and all, I think you'd make a good match for Alex."

"It would be good to be married to a doctor," Belinda finally said after a few moments. "At least, he wouldn't be like Arnie."

"Arnie?" Maryann asked.

"Yeah. My neighbor. He's always hanging around. Of course, he's good with the kids and all, but I figure, if I have a shot at a doctor, I should take it. My mother would be mad at me if I didn't. Arnie doesn't have much ambition."

"Do you mean he doesn't work?"

"Of course he works," Belinda said, looking offended. "He's a fine man. He works on one of the fishing boats. It's just that he's not a doctor or anything."

"He sounds like a good man to me."

"But I thought you wanted me to date the doctor," Belinda protested. "I can date Arnie any old time."

Maryann thought back to her mother's discontent in her various marriages. "Sometimes you just have to pick a good man and stay with him."

Belinda leaned back in her chair. "Are you sure you don't need me? You know I care about the children of this town as much as anyone. And this doctor is good to them. I've heard he tends to anyone who needs him, and he doesn't make them pay. At least not much. We want to keep him here if we can."

Maryann nodded. At least the gossips had adequately captured why she and her cousin were looking for someone for Alex. "He is a good doctor. But don't worry, I'll find someone else for him."

"Suzie Platter might be interested. I think she just broke up with Joe—you know? Joe Tribett?"

Maryann shook her head. "Maybe she'll join the choir Amy is getting together for the Christmas pageant."

"I don't think she sings."

"Neither does anyone else," Maryann said.

"Well, then maybe she will." With that bit

of optimistic news, Belinda stood up. "I better get home. Arnie is boiling eggs to make the kids some sandwiches for lunch tomorrow."

"Sounds like he's a keeper," Maryann said with a smile.

"I do kind of like him," Belinda admitted as she neared the door.

Maryann watched the other woman walk out of the office before she let her smile fade away. She shouldn't have been surprised when Belinda showed up at the clinic. When were people going to forget what she'd said last night at the diner? How could information travel so fast in this small town, when they didn't even have a newspaper? And—her heart sank—how badly had she messed things up with Alex? He might say it was okay, but had he really forgiven her? She'd gotten over being worried that he would fire her, but she was realizing she valued his good opinion above most anyone else's.

Chapter Four

Alex closed the door to the clinic. Dusk was quickly turning to dark, and Maryann was waiting for him on the porch. She'd walked back to her room at Lindy's Boarding House to change out of her uniform and into a pair of jeans. He flipped the sign on the door, so it showed the clinic was no longer open. The sign, like so many others in Treasure Creek, had the dark imprint of a moose on it.

It was growing colder by the second. Indoor lights had already been turned on in the nearby buildings, and the smell of wood fires drifted through the air.

"How's your brother?" Maryann asked as she pulled up the hood on her jacket and slipped her hands into her pockets. "He didn't have his usual questions when he called. I hope he's okay."

Alex hesitated and then told himself that, if he wanted to change Maryann's opinion about him being an ice man, he needed to open up more. Besides, he was a little worried about his brother. "Rocco has been saying he has something big to tell me for a while. He's getting agitated that I haven't gone to see him to talk in person. He won't say what it is, but today he added that he doesn't think I should leave Alaska. He says I should stay right here."

"Really?" Maryann looked up in surprise. "I thought he wanted you to come back to Los Angeles to live."

Alex nodded grimly as he held out his arm to Maryann. He didn't want her to stumble in the growing darkness. "He lives right in the middle of Duarte. That's the reason I'm going back there to build my clinic. I owe it to him. I'm not just dedicating the clinic in his name, I want him to feel like it's his. To have some place close enough for him to visit. Besides he's my brother. He needs me there."

"Well of course, your parents—"

Alex grunted. "My parents aren't even there most of the time. My mother's staying in Palm Springs right now, and my father is in Utah, going to some nutritional conferences. Since I got the attendant for Rocco, my parents are both traveling more. Which I thought would be good. Take the pressure off them. But it's like they've decided to divorce without taking the legal step. They didn't spend much time with Rocco before, anyway, but at least they were there in the house. Now he has been alone too much."

Maryann nodded and put her hand on his arm. Neither one of them started down the steps, though. Alex was noticing that a few strands of Maryann's hair had escaped when she pulled the rest of her glorious hair under her jacket hood. He felt like tucking the strays in, but he resisted the urge.

"Maybe he just meant you should stay here a few weeks longer," Maryann finally said. "That would make sense."

"Nothing makes sense," Alex muttered and then stopped. He wasn't sure what he was talking about any longer. He suddenly wondered if Maryann had ever gone for a moonlight walk down the road to where the log jam usually occurred on the creek. It would only be a mile past the boarding house where she stayed. When there were no street lamps, the sky was deep black and the stars even brighter. Of course, she couldn't go on that kind of a walk by herself; even he took flares with him to scare away any wild animals.

He mentally shook himself. The two of them alone in the dark together was a bad idea. He needed to remember he was leaving here and that the Northern nights played with people's emotions.

"Actually, Rocco was very clear," Alex said, bringing himself back to the conversation. He had no business wondering how much Maryann's brown eyes would deepen in the moonlight. "He thought I was moving back to take care of him and—"

"Well, aren't you?" Maryann asked when he stopped.

"Of course I am. I owe him everything. He saved my life."

"What do you mean?" she asked.

He suddenly found himself speaking of the accident and how his brother had been injured saving his life. Maryann said nothing, perhaps realizing how painful the memory was for him. She merely squeezed his arm in support as they continued walking in silence.

"I wish we weren't going to Amy's meeting," Alex finally said as they started walking on the edge of the asphalt. Light was spilling out from the businesses, many of them wood frame buildings with frontier facades, adding charm to their walk.

Maryann turned to face him and asked,

"It's because we're going to Lizbet's Diner, isn't it? By now, everyone in there must know what I said last night. Again, I'm so sorry."

The both stopped. They were in front of the Treasure Creek General Store. Alex looked through the display window and saw Harry Peters, the owner of the store, scowling at a fishing rod he was trying to hang on a rack. If anyone had been inside to listen to him, the middle-aged man would be complaining. The man did a lot of that lately, Alex realized.

"They don't call Harry an ice man, do they?" Alex suddenly wanted to know. He didn't want people to think he suffered the same disgruntledness that seemed to be part of the other man's life.

"No, they call him a curmudgeon," Mary-ann admitted with a slight smile. "You're the only ice man around that I know of."

Alex nodded as he rapped on the store's window with his knuckles. "That's good."

Harry peered at him a minute before giving him an unsmiling thumbs-up.

Alex nodded back. He supposed a thumbs-up was a start to having a happier day.

"Everyone knows what I said last night," Maryann muttered. "Even Harry thinks you're on a date—with *me*."

So that's what the store owner was saying

with his gesture. Alex looked over and saw the miserable look on Maryann's face. "Would that be so bad? Lots of people go on dates."

"It just feels awkward."

"It's okay. We'll just walk into Lizbet's and pretend last night never happened."

"Just like that?" She looked up at him skeptically. Even though they had stopped, she still had her hand on his right arm and he put his left hand over it. Her fingers were cold so he left his hand there to warm them up.

"I don't see how—" she continued.

He interrupted. "We'll make it fun."

Since Alex still had his hand on her fingers, he could feel the shock go through her.

"It's not like I never have fun," he said, defending himself softly, hoping she wouldn't ask him to give specific details. It was longer ago than he cared to remember. Probably the last time he'd laughed very much was when he'd been down to visit Rocco in the spring. It was now well into September.

Maryann nodded, but she didn't look convinced.

"Here." He lifted his hand and smoothed the wayward strands of hair under the hood of her jacket. Her cheeks were as smooth as he'd imagined. And her eyes opened wide enough in surprise that he had a glimpse of how she'd look when staring at the stars.

If he didn't get her to the diner soon, he'd kiss her right here in front of Harry's window. He didn't even want to count all of the reasons that would be a bad idea, although he had to say, it would definitely be fun. And it might give Harry some ideas of his own.

Alex cleared his throat. "Amy reserves the back room when we meet for dinner." His voice sounded hoarse.

Fortunately, Maryann didn't seem to notice his voice. She just started walking with him to Lizbet's.

Maryann pushed the jacket hood off her head as she and Alex stood under the diner's porch light. By now the sun had set and it was totally dark. She lifted her hands to puff her hair up a little. The hood had a tendency to squash it down, and she didn't want to look flat headed. Like fur-trimmed parkas, hair that was pressed down was a common sight around Alaska. At least for those people who liked to stay warm.

"You look good," Alex said as he smiled down at her.

She felt a tiny little tremble in her knees. It was to be expected, she supposed. Alex was so focused that everything he did was magnified. Even a look that meant nothing to him could make a woman feel special. She needed to keep her feet on the ground and remember that. "We need to look more businesslike if you want to avoid any teasing when we walk in."

They could smell the hamburgers being grilled and hear muffled laughter from the people inside. There was a window beside the door, and Maryann could see people sitting at tables in the dim light of the main dining room.

Alex grinned as he opened the door. "I could go around passing out those pamphlets we got from the CDC, urging everyone to get their flu shot this year."

"That would be better," Maryann agreed with a quick smile as she straightened her jacket. "They shouldn't tease a doctor, anyway. You care for the sick. They might need you someday."

If Maryann didn't believe she had to give Alex support because she was the one who had started all of the gossip, she would have turned around and said she'd decided to go home after all. She couldn't imagine what Amy would want from her at this meeting. That question had gone through her head all afternoon. There were dozens of new people in town who could give input into the kind of tours Amy's company should give. Besides, the woman needed to have a focus group and not rely on one opinion. Maryann hadn't noticed that anyone was complaining about the tours the company currently offered, anyway. It sure seemed to her that there was something for everyone's taste.

The chatter inside the diner didn't cease as Maryann stepped into the main room. The place was packed. People at several of the tables shared pizzas on tin trays that were elevated in the middle of their tables. Others had regular plates topped with sandwiches and hamburgers. She thought she smelled chili cooking in the kitchen, too.

"You know the way to the back room?" Alex asked her quietly.

She nodded. "I should have reserved it last night for dinner with my cousin. At least then no one would have heard us."

Alex chuckled. "You need a minimum of ten people to use the room. Trust me, one of the ten would have sold you out for a slice of pizza before you got out of here, anyway."

Maryann carefully wound her way through the gaps between the tables. Men with untrimmed beards and flannel shirts shared

tables with tourists in khaki pants, with base-
ball caps perched on their heads. She saw several of the fancy women sitting with some
of the local men. Joleen, the woman who'd
been so friendly this afternoon, looked up at
her as Maryann walked by, and nodded. The
woman was sharing a plate of nachos with a
man Maryann didn't know.

"Hi there." One of the fresh-faced waitresses waved to Maryann and Alex as they
walked by. "Need a table?"

"No, thanks, we're going to the back room,"
Alex said as he guided them past another few
tables.

"I wonder if she's the one who heard me
and my cousin talking," Maryann muttered
to Alex softly.

He smiled. "The way I hear it, all the waitresses took turns going over and listening.
Then they pooled what they heard. They
should work for the CIA."

The door to the back room was almost
closed, and light was shining out from around
its edges. Maryann was surprised she didn't
hear any noise on the other side of the door.
"I thought we would be a little late."

Alex pushed the door open.

"Surprise!" The call rang out and confet-
ti flew through the air. A "Happy Birthday

Alex." banner was strung across the far window, and colorful balloons were hanging from the ceiling. The walls of the room were paneled in oak, and tiny white lights outlined the windows. On a table underneath the banner was a double-tiered chocolate cake with unlit candles.

"Happy Birthday," one of the other tour guides, Nate McMann, said as he stepped closer to them and thumped Alex on the back. "Why didn't you say something? I would have taken you out to breakfast."

"I forgot my birthday's tomorrow," Alex said with a grin. "You've still got time."

"Breakfast?" Gage Parker, a tall, dark-haired tour guide, came over to stand by Maryann. He looked down at her with a grin. "I gave him a better gift than that. I sent the fancy women over to visit."

Maryann gasped. "*You* sent them? I thought *I* was responsible."

Gage was her cousin's new fiancée, and as smitten with love as any man Maryann had ever seen.

He grinned. "Well, I did use the words you and Karenna threw around to get the women motivated. Good work, by the way. Ten people told me about it before I saw Karenna. Nothing makes a man more appealing than knowing some woman is out looking for a match for him. Everyone's afraid they'll lose out if they don't act right away. It's like a clearance sale. Women fight to buy something they're not sure they want, just to be sure no one else gets it before they can decide if they do want it or not."

"Thanks a lot," Alex muttered. "You've just compared me to sheets and towels."

Gage shrugged with another grin. "Hey, you've got to give women what they want."

Maryann elbowed Gage. "My cousin didn't find you in the bargain basement, you know."

Gage grew suddenly serious. "I wouldn't have cared where she found me. Just that she did."

Maryann nodded. Karenna was the one member of the Jenner family who had managed to find true love without losing her mind completely.

By this time, Amy had walked up to Alex and given him a hug. After she greeted Alex, the other woman turned to Maryann. "I'm so glad you came. I knew Alex would want you here for his party, and I couldn't think of much of a reason to get you to come without spoiling the surprise." She paused. "Not that we don't want your input on the tours. We're always looking for more ideas."

"I didn't even know it was his birthday," Maryann confessed to the other woman. "And I'm his nurse."

"Don't worry about it," Amy said. "He never tells anyone something like that. I just know because he put it on his application for the tour guide job. I never ask the year, but I do ask the day. Besides, it's not until tomorrow."

Nate was slapping Alex on the back. "Maybe instead of breakfast, I should set you up with a date. I wouldn't want to be shown up by Gage. Just because he's found his happiness doesn't mean I can't come up with someone for you to date." Then Nate turned to Maryann. "Who was it you wanted him to date, anyway?"

"I don't really have anyone," Maryann stammered. "I mean, it's none of my business, anyway. And people need to find their own…" She spread her hands. "Anyway, I'm sorry I said anything."

Nate just laughed. "Don't worry about it. Alex here probably needed some encouragement." He turned to face his friend. "How old are you now?"

"Thirty-two, and I can find my own dates," Alex said with a grin. "And since we're on the subject, how many women came to see you today?"

"Okay, point taken," Nate said. "But you have to admit I live out of town so it's harder to get to my place. I'd have to draw the women a map."

"Well, you're here now, and I don't see them gathering around," Alex said.

Both men started to laugh.

Just then one of the waitresses came in carrying a tray of grilled hamburgers. There were plates of sliced tomatoes and onions on the side of the tray. Then another waitress walked in, carrying a tray with tall glasses of ice tea and water.

"Let's pray before we sit down," Amy invited them as she walked to the table that was set with silverware and napkins for everyone. She bowed her head. Everyone followed her lead.

"Father, we thank you for our good friend, Alex, here. Bless not just his birthday, but the rest of his life. And strengthen us with the food You provide. In Jesus' name, amen."

Amy looked around at the tour guides. "Before we sit down, I have an announcement. I expect you all to keep it confidential, but—as most of you know already—someone has stolen the treasure map."

Maryann knew of the map that Amy's great-great-grandfather had drawn, back when Treasure Creek was founded. It supposedly led to a valuable treasure. Since Amy's two young boys had found the map a few months ago, it and its treasure had been the talk of the town.

She looked at Alex. "Do you think there is real treasure buried around here?"

Alex shrugged as he pulled out a chair for her. "I suspect whoever has that map hopes there is gold. And who knows? It does sound like there was treasure at some point, because Amy remembers her grandfather saying his father had said the treasure should only be sought if their family ever had 'dire times.' That sounds like gold to me."

Maryann stopped. "What did you say?"

"That sounds like gold to me."

"No, the dire times. Were those the exact words?"

Alex nodded. By now, everyone else had been seated at the table, and they were look-ing at them. "Why?"

Maryann looked over at Amy. "I think I know where your map is. When Timmy Fields was at the clinic this morning he said something about dire times and I noticed he'd slipped an old sheet of paper into the Bible I'd given him to hold."

Amy gasped. "He was over playing with my sons before the map disappeared. My boys know about the prediction for dire times. It's an old family story."

"Timmy must know then, too. He was found along the Chilkoot Pass."

"I was afraid something like this would happen. The poor boy could have died out there, looking for that treasure," Amy said.

"And he probably only wanted to help out his parents," Maryann said. "They're certainly hurting for money, now that his father is out of a job."

"Dire times." Amy nodded. "There's a lot of that around here these days. Treasure Creek has really struggled economically since Ben died and the tour business took a hit."

"I can walk back to the clinic and get the map for you right now." Alex started to rise from his chair.

"Certainly not," Amy said, as she motioned for him to sit. "It can wait. We're going to eat and have some of your cake. If that map's locked up in your clinic, it isn't going any-where—tonight anyway."

* * *

An hour later, Alex looked around the room
and decided he was a contented man. Even
the few good-natured jibes about him and the
fancy women didn't trouble him. In fact, he
had started rather enjoying them, once Maryann began to turn pink every time someone
mentioned the women.

"You're a good sport," he said to her quietly.
They'd both finished their hamburgers and
fries. "No one blames you for those women
showing up today in the clinic. The guys were
just having fun."

Maryann shrugged and smiled with her
brown eyes. "I figure they'll stop joking when
they get a piece of your birthday cake."

Alex chuckled and put an arm on the back
of her chair so he could lean in and lower his
voice even more. "I wouldn't count on it. I've
seen these guys in action. They know how
to out-wait a polar bear in spring thaw. They
just don't let go when they have something on
their mind."

Alex hadn't thought about it before he put
his arm on her chair. But once it was there,
he didn't want to move it away. The table
was crowded and their chairs were close
enough together that he hoped it didn't look
like he was putting his arm around her. At

least Maryann didn't seem to take it that way, although he did notice a slight frown forming on her face.

"You don't see polar bears on those tours you take, do you?" she asked him in alarm. "That doesn't seem very safe. You could be hurt."

"Eaten alive," he confirmed cheerfully. "Although it's usually the grizzlies that do that."

Her eyes grew wider still.

Alex couldn't remember the last time someone had worried about him. He shouldn't tease her about this. "Actually, I do the bus tours— basically following the White Pass Trail, with stops at every photo op we can find. Some of the guides are experienced enough to go after the wild animals, but not me. The scariest things I'm likely to see are mosquitoes. "

"Well, that's good," Maryann said as she settled back into her chair.

The instant she leaned back far enough for her neck to touch his arm, she stiffened. Alex didn't move; he didn't even breathe. The skin at the back of her neck was soft and felt vulnerable. Gradually, he felt Maryann relax against his arm. She accepted him. He wished he'd put his arm there sooner.

Just then, Amy stood up at the front of the

table. When she had everyone's attention, she lifted her hands to lead everyone in singing "Happy Birthday" to him. Alex wished they would finish the song as quickly as possible. He wasn't used to this kind of attention, with everyone looking at him.

Of course, the other guides had to add some offbeat verses to the birthday song, so they could keep singing. On the second time around, Alex surprised himself by blinking. His eyes were moist; he was suddenly realizing that he was going to miss this little northern town when he went back to Los Angeles.

He blinked again. When he'd first come to Treasure Creek, he couldn't wait to leave. He had bristled at the high cost of everything that had to be shipped in or flown down from Anchorage. The summer days were too long, and he never thought he'd adjust to the brief episodes of gray light people here called daytime in the winter months.

But he had friends here. He'd been so busy with med school that he hadn't had a normal life for years. He didn't want to tell these friends, but this was the first party he'd had in years. Usually, he got a congratulatory call from Rocco, and that was it. His parents had given up marking his birthday when he'd left for college. Even before that, there had been so much isolation and sadness in his family, a celebration had never seemed quite appropriate for holidays or birthdays.

"Alex?" He heard Maryann quietly speaking his name, and he realized he'd been lost in thought.

"Huh?"

"Amy asked if you'd made your birthday wish yet?"

He saw the waitress use a match to light the candles on his cake. He'd forgotten about the tradition of a wish. It didn't take more than a second, though, for him to know what his was. It was a foolish desire, but then this was a childish game. So he nodded. He wished he could stay right here in Treasure Creek and get to know Maryann better.

Someone dimmed the lights and the waitress who had lit the candles brought the cake to him so he could blow them out. Before he did, he took a moment to see how Maryann's eyes looked in candlelight. They were dazzling.

Maybe that was enough good to come from a birthday wish.

Something was happening to him, he realized. His hands felt clammy and his breathing was suddenly a little labored. He wondered if he was coming down with something.

"What's wrong?" Maryann asked. Her brown eyes deepened.

"Nothing," Alex said. And there wasn't really anything amiss except that he so enjoyed looking at her.

"Go ahead, blow out your candles," Maryann finally said. "People are starting to look at you funny."

Alex leaned forward so much that his arm left the back of Maryann's chair and slid up to her shoulder. Then, with what breath he had left, he blew out his candles.

When he finished, he looked around at the other tour guides. They were staring at him like he'd changed into an alien right before their eyes. And, of course, he had. He'd started to show his emotions. The blinking had fooled no one. And the arm he had around Maryann's shoulders revealed that this was almost a date in his mind. If he ever had been an ice man, he was thawing. Of course, it couldn't be happening at a worse time. His heart might tell him to stay in Treasure Creek, but his duty lay back in Los Angeles with his brother.

It was a comfort to know that the guides sitting around this table were not strangers to that kind of duty. Gage had taken his brother's son into his home when his brother couldn't care for him. Another guide was supporting his invalid mother. They had all rallied around Amy when her husband died. A man didn't just think of himself in this life. Not if he lived in Treasure Creek. Each of them had put someone else's needs before their own, at some time since he'd known them.

Which didn't explain why all of them were quiet right now. He was an easy target, sitting there. Ordinarily, at least one of the guides would make a joke about his wandering arm. Or his birthday wish. But they were all as somber as he was. Which, when he realized it, only told him how bad off they thought he was.

The waitress had cut the birthday cake and she gave him the first piece. He passed it on to Maryann. If he was thawing, it was because of her. Something about her had gotten to him. Not that it was likely to last beyond the night. He nodded his thanks when the waitress silently gave him a second piece of cake. Tomorrow, in the clear light of day, he'd be back at his desk, going about his routine, knowing he'd leave for Los Angeles in three weeks and never look back. It's what he had to do.

Just thinking about it made the cake taste like straw.

He looked over at Amy. "I'll slip back to the clinic and get that map for you." He set his fork back on the plate. "It'll only take a few minutes."

He could use the walk, he told himself. The cold air would remind him that nights like this weren't made for him, at least not until he'd finished building that clinic. Maybe once the place was up and running, he could leave it with his staff long enough for him to come back here for a few months some summer.

As he stood he found Amy looking at him with a small, secret smile on her face, and he didn't know what it meant.

"It's your birthday." Amy said. "When you finish your cake, why don't you walk Maryann home? I'll come by the clinic tomorrow morning to get the map. The stars are beautiful tonight. It'd be a shame to waste them."

Now he knew what that look meant. Amy had been as close as a sister to him and he appreciated her approval. Maybe he should take a chance. He slid his plate of cake back further on the table. Maryann had finished hers.

"How about it?" he asked Maryann.

She nodded. "I wouldn't mind getting home early tonight."

He and Maryann said quick goodbyes and were out in the evening air before Alex had time to realize what he was doing.

Alex watched Maryann pull on her jacket hood again. "You don't have gloves with you, do you?"

She shook her head. "I forgot them back at my room."

"Well," Alex said, blessing the forgetfulness that was so unlike her, "I can fix that."

He took his right hand out of his pocket and offered it to her. "I don't have my gloves either."

She took his hand.

Alex felt the warmth of her hand as his covered Maryann's. Then she slipped her other hand into her pocket. She had her chin down and he wondered if it was possible she was shy. The night seemed a bit less chilly now as they stepped off the porch together.

The stars were plentiful tonight. In a month or two anyone walking in their steps would have a chance of seeing the northern lights. But, for now, the deep soft black of the night was enough. He wondered if Maryann felt any of the emotions he felt, stirring inside him.

"There's a moose," she whispered as she

took her other hand out of her pocket and pointed. "By that old building."

Sure enough, the moose was there, standing perfectly still, outlined in the night. And then, as they stood and watched, the big bull majestically strolled down the road out of town.

"Wow," Maryann whispered in awe. "I'd never seen anything like that until I came up here."

"Me neither." Alex nodded. She had no reason to know, he told himself, that he was looking at her instead of the moose. Her whole face was filled with joy. As had his heart.

Maryann didn't know what she saw in his face, but her eyes widened as though she was surprised by it.

"Do you think he'll stay?" she asked, and it took Alex a few seconds to realize she meant the moose.

Maryann turned her face away from him slightly and the night shadows covered her eyes with darkness.

"I'm sure he wishes he could," Alex finally said.

He doubted she recognized the longing in his voice, but she looked at him fully this time. Her eyes held a hint of sympathy, and some emotion he could not identify. The combination of the two was his undoing.

He kept his eyes trained on hers, looking for any sign that she was uncomfortable as he leaned down. Her lips were soft. He knew he should stop the kiss, but he couldn't. He was leaving; he didn't deserve a kiss like this. But he was helpless to end it. He wondered if the northern lights weren't coming out early after all. Something around him seemed to light up the night.

Chapter Five

Maryann snuggled deeper into the covers of her bed. Light frost was on the square-paned window and she could hear the sputter of the old radiator heater as it struggled to raise the temperature in her cold room. She felt a warm contentment inside and wondered vaguely if it was Sunday morning. Usually Lindy, the owner of the boarding house, would be up and brewing coffee to lure everyone down the hall to the dining room. But the sky was dark and Maryann closed her eyes again, luxuriating in the knowledge that she didn't have to put her feet on the chilly wooden floor just yet. She had time to lie here and anticipate another perfect day in paradise.

Then it hit her. Her eyes popped wide open. Alex had kissed her, and she'd wanted him to. It was a foolish mistake on her part. He was leaving. She would be as unlucky in love as her parents were.

Not that she had been in love last night, she assured herself quickly. Temporarily insane maybe, but not in love.

She closed her eyes and willed the sun to stop rising. Nothing could black out her memory, though. She drew in her breath before she could even think the words.

Last night she'd kissed her boss.

It wasn't quite dawn yet, but it would be soon. In the dim light, Maryann looked around the small room. An old mirror hung over an oak dresser and there was a sitting chair by the window. Too many of her belongings were still in the boxes she'd had sent up from Spokane.

For the first time since she'd come racing up to Treasure Creek—following her cousin, who'd driven up here in her bridal gown after her wedding had failed to happen—Maryann questioned whether she should stay. No one in her family seemed able to have a calm, measured courtship. Maryann wanted to be the exception. This little town had seemed like such a peaceful oasis. She'd thought she would be free of chaos and drama here.

She forced herself to start breathing slower. She needed to calm down. It was a kiss; she hadn't murdered anyone or embezzled money or assaulted a policeman. Her embarrassment might be uncomfortable, but it would fade.

Maryann swung her feet around and set them down on the braided rug by her bed. If she could, she needed to get to the clinic before Alex did. It would feel less uncomfortable to see him if she was filing out a chart than if she was just sitting there when he came in. She stood on the rug and then quickly hopped along the cold floor to the closet, where she pulled out a clean white uniform. First the slacks and then a top.

She threw the clothes on the bed and raced back to the rug. Only a very small percentage of nurses still wore white uniforms. That's how traditional she was. There were no large flowers or laughing clowns on her clothes.

She didn't deserve to be overtaken by drama like this.

Maybe Alex wouldn't even mention the kiss.

Alex turned his key in the front door to the clinic. He'd decided to walk over from the house he rented on the far edge of town. Already, there had been a note stuck in his door this morning, from someone asking if he could put in a good word for them with his landlord. His was one of the few rentals in Treasure Creek, and everyone knew he would vacate it soon. Most people who moved here had to stay at the boarding house for a while, like Maryann was doing.

There he went again. He'd already noticed this morning that every thought that sprang to his mind somehow took him back to Maryann. Which was why he'd come over to the clinic early. He had a stack of medical journals to read. Usually, when he was reading them, nothing else mattered. They were his escape.

He'd barely put his feet up on his desk and leaned his chair back when he heard a knock on the clinic door. They weren't scheduled to open for another half hour, but he knew it might be an emergency, so he put his journal down and walked out of his office into the hall.

"Coming," he called out, as he made his way to the door. He wondered if Maryann had lost her key.

When he opened the door, it was Amy.

"Oh," he said as he stood to the side so she could come in. "Good morning."

"You thought I was someone else, didn't you?" she asked as she loosened the scarf she had wrapped around her neck. She stood in the open doorway with an unrepentant grin on her face.

"I did think you might be Maryann," he agreed calmly.

"I knew it," Amy said in triumph as she stepped inside and walked over to the chairs. "The two of you—"

"She works here. Of course, I thought it was her." He stood there, holding the door without moving. He wasn't going to give an inch. Not the way gossip spread around this town.

"Last night, I thought—"

"She and I have no future," Alex said, interrupting his well-meaning friend. "Remember, I'm leaving at the end of the month."

Just then he heard tentative footsteps on the porch. He looked over his shoulder. It was Maryann, and she'd clearly heard everything he just said.

"Good morning," Maryann said as she finished walking across the porch without making eye contact.

Oh, he was smooth all right, Alex told himself. He heard Maryann greet Amy with more warmth than she'd managed to do with him.

Finally, he remembered to close the door.

"You must be here about the map," Maryann said to Amy as she unsnapped her jacket and hung it on the hook behind the reception desk.

Amy nodded. "I thought Alex and you might have forgotten."

Please, dear Lord, Alex thought, *don't let Amy go into her explanation of why she thought he and Maryann would have forgotten.* He had the prayer finished before he realized it was the first time he'd prayed in decades. God probably wasn't very impressed with him. Amy stayed silent though, so God must still be merciful to fools and desperate men.

"I'll go get the map now," Alex said with as much dignity as he could muster. "It's on the shelf in our exam room."

"No, I can get it," Maryann insisted and turned. "You two sit down and figure out how you're going to handle telling Timmy we found the map.

"I didn't think of that," Alex said as he sat down. He shouldn't be surprised that Maryann saw through to the heart of the problem quicker than he had. He might know the names of more diseases, but she was an instinctive healer.

He didn't breathe easy until his nurse had gone down the hall and entered the office.

"We'll have to call the Fields," Alex said as he turned to look over at Amy. "Maybe Timmy will talk to us on the phone and we can explain that we have to put the map back where it belongs. He's old enough to understand that."

Amy nodded thoughtfully. "I know he didn't mean any harm, but I don't want him to think it is okay to take things that belong to other people."

"Yes, of course," Alex said, nodding.

Maryann came back with the white Bible, and, standing in front of them, opened it.

"That's it," Amy cried, relieved, as she reached for the old yellow paper that was folded between the pages.

"Poor Timmy. He wouldn't have started out looking for that treasure if he didn't think it would help his family," Maryann agreed quietly. "I bet he feels just terrible."

Maryann looked up at Alex, her eyes so full of concern for the boy that he knew she'd forgotten her earlier coldness to him. He smiled back. "It would be best if Timmy could give the map back. Like you said, I'm sure he must be feeling guilty that he took it. At least he should have a chance to make it right."

Alex knew more about guilt than most people, and he knew it was important for a man—or a boy—to face what he had done wrong and make amends. It was the only thing that brought healing. Alex looked forward to the day when he could say he'd made his own amends.

"You're absolutely right," Amy said, as she laid the map back down in the open Bible. "I'll wait for Timmy to return it to me."

"I could make a copy of it if you want," Maryann offered. "You wouldn't want to lose it. You might find the treasure."

Amy smiled. "There's no denying I could use some financial help, but the map is more than just some directions to a treasure. I like holding the piece of paper and thinking of my great-great-grandfather drawing it with his family in mind. It makes me feel so connected to the past. Like someone cared about me before I was even born. I wonder what he would have thought of me if he'd had a chance to know me?"

"He would have thought you are one gracious lady," Maryann said firmly before Alex had a chance to respond. Then she sat down beside Amy, the open Bible on her lap. "Not everyone would risk losing a treasure map to make a boy feel better."

They were all silent for a moment.

"Well, I should go to my office and call the Fields," Alex finally said. "With all those kids, I'm sure they're awake by now. Probably ready for a nap, in fact."

"I expect so," Maryann agreed.

He noticed she'd stopped looking at him again. They needed to sit down and talk. Maybe after Amy left there would be a chance. He didn't quite know what he would say, but they couldn't leave things the way they were.

Maryann watched Alex walk down the hall and open the door to his office. Once he was inside, she didn't even try to hide her misery.

"Trouble?" Amy reached out and put a hand on her on her leg.

Maryann shrugged as she looked over at her. "I get myself in some messes."

"Well, we all do," Amy said. "Want to talk about it?"

Maryann shook her head. "It's okay. It's just that things have been so peaceful here, you know, and then—well, I need to get myself grounded again. That's all."

Suddenly Alex came charging back to the waiting room and all thought of being grounded fled Maryann's mind. He had his black medical bag in his hand, the one with the double silver snaps that he kept for emergencies.

"I need to get out to the Fields's place," Alex announced as he reached for the coat he'd left on the rack by the door. He looked at Maryann, all traces of his earlier uncertainty gone. "Timmy's burning up with fever."

"Oh no," Maryann said, and stood up. "I thought they were supposed to let us know if he had a high temperature."

"It wasn't so bad yesterday afternoon, they said. So they decided not to come back," Alex said as he opened his bag and started checking the medications he had. "Timmy kept saying he needed to come back to the doctor's, but they said he wasn't sick enough. So the little fool went outside last night to get sicker. And now—" Alex turned to her. "I could only listen to his breathing on the phone, but it worries me. I didn't want to ask the parents to bring him in, because I wasn't sure they would. There was something about the pickup, and Mr. Fields doesn't want to take on more debt, he says. I told him there'd be no charge, but he still didn't seem convinced."

Maryann walked to the hook behind her

desk and took down her coat. "You might need help."

Alex looked up at her. "Thanks."

"I'll put a sign on the door saying we've gone on an emergency." Maryann found a piece of white paper on her desk and picked up a black marker.

"We should be back in an hour," Alex said. "I'll check Timmy out and leave some anti-biotics for him to take. If that's not enough, we'll need to decide what to do then."

Maryann made the sign for the door and picked up her roll of tape, walking across the waiting room to the door.

"Here, let me get that," Amy said, as she met Maryann at the door and opened it.

"Thanks." Maryann pulled off a piece of tape and used it to attach the sheet of paper to the wood of the door. Then she turned around. Alex was at the door by now, too.

Alex looked at Amy. "Could you let Dr. Logan know I'm going to see the Fields? Just in case any of my patients go to him when they see I'm not here."

Amy nodded and then held out the Bible in her hand to both of them. "Timmy will want this."

Maryann noticed the yellowed paper peek-

ing out from the pages, just as it had been
when Timmy put it there.

"You don't really need to do that," Maryann
said softly. "It's your map. We can keep it here
if you want."

Amy smiled. "Timmy can give it back
when he feels better. I think my great-great-
grandfather would want me to do this."

Maryann nodded. "I'll see that he takes
good care of it, then."

With that, she and Alex headed out.

"We'll take my Jeep," Alex said as they
stepped off the porch.

Maryann nodded. She'd never ridden with
Alex in his Jeep.

They walked quickly up the road until they
reached the house where Alex lived. The house
had once belonged to a single family, but it
had been divided into apartments years ago.
Maryann knew all about that house. Several
people had already suggested she ask Alex to
put in a good word for her with his landlord
so she'd be in line to get his apartment when
he left.

Maryann remembered to pay attention
when they walked by the house. New white
paint and green trim. It looked well main-
tained, and that was important in Alaska, as
that meant things like the heating system were

probably up-to-date, too. And the plumbing, which could be difficult when the ground was frozen.

"Nice curtains," Maryann said as Alex unlocked the passenger door of his Jeep.

He grunted in response as he opened the door, and stood there waiting for her.

Maryann climbed inside. The passenger seat was high because the whole vehicle set up off the road more than normal cars. She knew from what people said that the doctor's Jeep had a special four-wheel drive...something. He used it when he went to the Taiya village to preside over a health clinic.

"The road that goes to the Fields place is the one that follows the Dyea River through the valley," Alex said as he started the Jeep. "I hope you don't mind a few bumps. I'm worried about that boy. There's no way to get over that gravel road fast without bouncing a bit."

"Don't worry about me," Maryann said. "Drive as fast as you can."

Alex nodded as he backed his Jeep out onto the road.

"Do you mind if I pray?" Maryann asked.

He shrugged and she took that as permission, so she bowed her head right then. She could have prayed silently, but the Bible said that when two were gathered together in prayer everything was stronger.

"God," she began quietly, *"You have given Timmy every breath He has ever taken. We pray You will protect his body from the fever that is taking hold of him. Help us get to his home quickly, so we can help him. Be with us all today, Father. In Jesus' name. Amen."*

"Amen," Alex agreed softly as he kept his eyes on the road.

Maryann was surprised. "Amen? I thought you don't believe in prayer anymore."

"I don't really," Alex answered ruefully as he turned off the asphalt road onto one that was little more than a rutted path. Wild grass grew in clumps and threatened to overgrow the dirt tracks that led the way back to the base of the mountain. "It's just that the words sound so hopeful, I can't help but agree."

"Maybe you believe more than you think you do, then." She continued to look at him. This untamed country seemed to suit him. He had a half smile on his lips as he concentrated on the ruts in front of them.

"Well, for now, let's just say I don't mind other people praying."

They were both silent for a few minutes

"I meant to say happy birthday this

morning," Maryann finally said, softly. "Since this is the day."

"Thank you," Alex said as he down-shifted gears to go up a small rise. "I appreciate it."

"I don't have a card," Maryann confessed. "I thought I'd go over to Harry's store during my lunch, and see if he has any."

"You don't need to get me one," Alex said. "Besides, neither one of us will get much time for lunch today."

Maryann decided not to press the point. She certainly didn't want him to think that he owed her any explanations about his life, just because he'd walked her home last night.

The Jeep went over a big bump, and she would have hit her head on the roof if she hadn't been wearing a seat belt.

"Is there homesteading out here?" Maryann asked, changing the subject. She knew that some of the more isolated areas in Alaska had been open to homesteaders until recently.

Alex shook his head. "Believe it or not, this isn't remote enough for that."

Maryann loved the wild nature of Alaska, but she had to admit, she wouldn't want to live out in the brush like this. Especially not when the bears woke from their winter hibernation and were hungry.

"The Fields place is just around this bend,"

Alex said. "I had to bring some medicine up here for Timmy one other time."

"Now, see? That's why you can't leave," Maryann said without thinking. "What other doctor would do that?"

Maryann wished she could call the words back the minute they left her mouth. "Not that I—I mean, I know you're leaving. It's your decision. Los Angeles must be a wonderful place to live."

"It's the pits," Alex said, sounding friendly enough. "At least the area around my parent's house is. It wasn't always that way, but they've lived there long enough for the stable homeowners to leave and landlords to buy the surrounding houses to rent out."

"Everything changes," Maryann murmured when he didn't say anything more. That was a comforting thought to her this morning. She needed to rein in her feelings about Alex; and she could, since even she could change.

"We're here," Alex announced as he pulled his Jeep to a stop.

A ramshackle house sprung up in front of her like a mirage. Different shades of siding covered the small square house in no discernible pattern. A mud-spattered white pickup of uncertain age was parked in front of the house. A bike with its front wheel off leaned against the corner of the house.

"They didn't hear us," Maryann said as she reached up to undo her seat belt buckle.

Alex rolled down his window. "Kids."

Maryann nodded. She could hear the screeching sounds. It didn't sound like anyone was injured, though—it was more like they were playing some game at the top of their lungs.

Alex opened his door and Maryann opened hers. He grabbed his medical bag and she took the Bible. The bite of the wind hit her in the face when she stepped out of the Jeep. She would have guessed that the vehicle kept very little of the wind away from its passengers, but she would have been mistaken. It was blowing fiercely out here.

They walked to the door of the house and knocked. Someone moved a curtain aside so they could look out the window. It was Timmy's father.

"I'm so glad it's you, Doctor," Mr. Fields said as he swung the door wide open.

The inside of the house was so hot it was suffocating. A couch covered with a pink Afghan was the main piece of furniture. The rest of the small room was filled with toys and children.

"I'm running out of ideas to try on Timmy, and he doesn't seem to be getting any better," the man said as he started heading down the hallway. "I tried to get the pickup going, but the battery is dead. He's having such a hard time breathing. I thought I'd take him to his mom, but she's at work. Then I was going to take him over to your place. I changed my mind after your call."

Mr. Fields opened the door to a small bedroom. A brown wool blanket was hanging over the only window and it blocked most of the sunshine from outside. Maryann could hear the labored breathing of Timmy, who was lying in the only bed in the room.

"Is he sensitive to light?" Alex asked as he stepped inside and walked toward the bed.

The room smelled of menthol and there was a blue jar of rubbing ointment on a metal nightstand, along with a couple of damp washcloths.

"He didn't complain about the light," Mr. Fields admitted. "I just thought it might be a problem. He was real sensitive to the light when he had measles a year ago."

"Take the blanket down then," Alex said as he set his medical bag on a straight-back chair near the bed. "Nurse Jenner and I will want to get a good look at Timmy."

"Do you have any ice?" Maryann turned to Mr. Fields as he swept the blanket off the curtain rods. Light flooded the cluttered room.

Mr. Fields looked up at her and nodded. "I'll get you some."

Maryann stood by as Alex listened to Timmy's lungs through his stethoscope. The boy's eyes were closed and his face was flushed.

"You okay, Timmy?" Maryann whispered as she stepped closer. The boy didn't open his eyes to look at her. She didn't think he even heard her. He was such a lively boy ordinarily, that she knew he was very sick.

Alex turned to look up at her. "We need to get him to a hospital."

Maryann heard a gasp from the doorway, so she turned.

"We can't afford a hospital," Mr. Fields protested. He had a ragged dishtowel draped over one arm and a metal bowl filled with ice cubes in the other.

Maryann could tell by his eyes that he was frightened.

"Can't we just take him to your clinic?" Mr. Fields asked.

"I don't have the same equipment as the hospital," Alex replied calmly. "We don't have a choice."

Maryann was already gathering up some of

the blankets on Timmy's bed. The first step
to getting the boy to the hospital was to put
him in the Jeep and drive him back to Treasure Creek. They'd need lots of blankets to
keep him comfortable for that part of the ride.
She was glad Alex was there to convince Mr.
Fields his son would need to go to Juneau.
That was the nearest hospital, and they had
a good pulmonary department. She wasn't a
doctor, but she could see how Timmy labored
to breathe.

"He needs a hospital," Alex repeated. "It's
important."

"Are you saying he might die?" Mr. Fields
whispered hoarsely.

Alex snapped his medical bag shut and
looked up at his patient's father. "I'm saying
we can't take that chance."

Mr. Fields looked at Maryann imploringly.
"I have to stay with my other children. Timmy
said he liked you. He called you his angel.
Don't let him die."

"We'll do all we can," Maryann assured
him. "Dr. Havens is a very good doctor."

Mr. Fields nodded. "You still got that
Bible?"

Maryann nodded as she put her hand on it.
She had slipped it into her pocket earlier, so
she could use her hands.

"Say a prayer over my Timmy," Mr. Fields said. "He likes the Twenty-third Psalm. Could you read it to him?"

Maryann nodded. "I will when he wakes up."

A slight moan came from the bed. The boy was starting to thrash around.

"And pray for that doctor of yours, too," Mr. Fields added quietly.

"I—" Maryann started to protest that he wasn't her doctor and then she stopped. Until the boy was doing better, she needed to put any of her personal feelings aside. She was a nurse. "Of course, I'll pray for everyone who takes care of Timmy."

She looked over at Alex. He was concentrating so hard on listening to Timmy breathing, he hadn't even heard her conversation with Mr. Fields. She wondered how he would feel about her praying for him.

Chapter Six

Alex looked up from where he was crouched beside Timmy's bed. "Is there a phone?"

Maryann recognized the resolve in Alex's demeanor. He'd decided what needed to be done, and now he was just taking the steps. She could see why that kind of focus could be misinterpreted to be coldness. But that wasn't what it meant at all. He was merely determined to do everything in his power to help his patients.

"In the kitchen," Mr. Fields replied a little reluctantly. "By the refrigerator."

"Mind if I use it?" Alex stood and turned to the door.

"Feel free," Mr. Fields said, but Alex was already stepping out of the room.

Maryann watched him walk away.

"I hope it's not a long-distance call," Mr.

Fields muttered when Alex was gone. Then he turned to Maryann. "I know how that sounds, but you've got to understand. A man like me—I don't have much. I want to take care of my family, but there's only so much I can do. I need help."

"I know, Mr. Fields," Maryann said as she stepped closer to pat his shoulder. She did feel sorry for the man. It's just that it was that kind of talk that had put them in this situation. "You might not want to worry the children, though. Timmy was trying to do just that— help you."

"Timmy?" the man stepped back in surprise. "How could he help? He's a kid."

"Maybe when this is all over, he'll tell you," Maryann said. "But for now, Timmy needs to be in the hospital. Dr. Havens wouldn't take him if it wasn't necessary."

Mr. Fields nodded. "I know. He's a good man."

Just then Alex came back into the room. "We're ready. Max O'Brian will fly us to Juneau." Alex looked at Mr. Fields. "He's not going to charge anything for the flight. He said he needs to fly there to pick up a passenger anyway, but we need to get back to Treasure Creek right away so we can go with him."

"Is there room for the missus?" Mr. Fields

asked. "She'll want to go. And one of us has to stay with the other kids. But someone needs to be there with our Timmy."

Alex nodded. "Call her and tell her to meet us at Max's in twenty minutes. I'm afraid there's no time for her to drive out here and pack a suitcase."

"I'll call her," Mr. Fields said.

With that, Alex scooped Timmy up with half of his blankets. Maryann followed them out with the other half of the blankets in her arms. The wind hit her when she stepped out of the house. Surely, it was too early for winter weather, she thought to herself. It wasn't even October yet. She knew Fairbanks usually had snow this time of the year, but that wasn't true for Treasure Creek.

Maryann hurried to the Jeep so she could open the door for Alex. She shook out several blankets and laid them wide against the small backseat. Alex bent down and laid Timmy in the middle of the blankets and then wrapped the ends around him.

"Should I ride back there with him?" Maryann asked.

"If you don't mind," Alex said. "I think it's good if someone talks to him so he knows we're here."

Maryann lifted Timmy slightly and climbed

into the seat so she could hold his head on her lap. She put her hand on his forehead. He was burning up with fever. She looked up at Alex, who was still standing in the open door. "I'm worried."

He nodded. "Me, too."

And then he shut the door.

When Alex started the Jeep, Maryann shifted herself so she would protect Timmy from the jarring movement caused by any of the bumps they might run into as they drove back to town. The Bible in her pocket pressed against the side of the Jeep. She'd squeezed into the back with Timmy, and there wasn't much room. She slipped a hand around and took the book out of her pocket. When she saw the yellowed edges of that old treasure map, she shook her head. No one was worried about that right now.

Holding the Bible reminded her of what she needed to do. She bowed her head and silently asked God to keep them in His hands. And then she began to quote one of the few sections of the Bible that she knew by heart. "Our Father, who are in Heaven, hallowed be thy name—"

Timmy moaned in her lap. She wasn't sure if he was trying to say that the prayer comforted him or distressed him. Maybe he thought it meant he was in danger of dying.

"It's all right," she murmured. "You're going to be just fine." Then she looked up and met Alex's eyes as he looked in the rearview mirror. "Dr. Havens is going to take really good care of you."

Alex stopped looking in the mirror and accelerated the Jeep slightly.

"We're almost to the asphalt road," he said.

Maryann nodded as she continued to rub Timmy's head.

Alex slowed down to take the turn by the creek. The water was still running, and anytime he drove by water, especially in the early morning hours, he knew to watch for animals. It would be a little late for them to be coming to drink today, but he didn't want to take any chances.

He knew Max would be ready to take off and that there was little time to spare. He was kicking himself for not calling Mr. Fields yesterday, after the clinic closed. If he had thought it through, he would have known something more than usual was wrong at the house because Mr. Fields had said he'd be back to start on the shelves, but then never appeared.

Alex figured that, if he had called, he could have talked to Timmy. Maybe if he'd talked to the boy, Timmy would have mentioned that map and he wouldn't have tried that fool stunt of trying to get sicker so his parents would bring him to the clinic.

Alex shook his head. He knew he wasn't responsible for missing things like that, but they always hit him hard anyway. Life seemed so out of control sometimes. He supposed he was still trying to find a way to make his peace with what he hadn't done when he was in that crosswalk with his brother so many years ago. He'd gone over that day so many times in his life, wondering what he could have done to change the events.

"We're almost there," Alex said as they neared Treasure Creek. In a mile or so, the road to the hangar where Max kept his float-plane would be off to his left. If the plane wasn't in the hangar, Max would have already brought it down to the dock where he loaded before takeoff. He hoped Mrs. Fields would already be around there somewhere. She worked at one of the hotels in town, so she'd be close enough to have arrived already if she got the message from her husband.

"I guess I haven't asked, but can you come with us?" Alex looked in the rearview mirror as he asked Maryann. "Max can probably fly you back when he meets his passenger for the return trip if you want, so you won't need to spend the night. I don't know how long Timmy will have to stay in the hospital."

Maryann nodded and swallowed. Then she met his eyes in the mirror.

"I've been wondering," she said hesitantly. "I know he needs to be in the hospital. But will they take him? Without insurance? I don't know how they do things up here, but in Spokane it would depend. It's not a heart attack or a gunshot wound."

"If you want to pray, that's what you need to pray for," Alex said, his mouth turning grim as his eyes met hers. "I don't know what they'll say. I just know he needs to be there."

Alex had thought Maryann would be pleased that he asked her to pray for something. He'd been sincere when he'd told her earlier that he had nothing against people praying. He had nothing against people howling at the moon either. He just didn't think either one of them changed the way things were. But he didn't see the smile he expected on Maryann's face. In fact her chin had gotten that slightly stubborn expression he'd noticed a time or two.

"Is there a problem?" he asked her.

"It's just that prayer works better if two people agree together on something," she said, her voice a little lofty. "I don't mind being one of the people, but I can't be both of them."

"Oh," he said. "Well, I can't help thinking someone else would do better at agreeing with you than I would."

The minute the words left his mouth, he realized they were wrong. "I mean, of course, I agree with you about many things. Especially getting Timmy into the hospital. But I don't need to pray to agree. Maybe Mrs. Fields will pray with you."

"That would work fine," Maryann said.

Now, why did he get the impression that she was trying to put him in his place?

"Some fine minds don't believe in prayer," he said in his defense.

"Yes, and those people are miserable fools," Maryann snapped back. "I don't care how fine you think their minds are. They're missing out on peace. Eternal, everlasting peace—so there."

He could never tell her, but she was cute when she got worked up about something.

"There's Mrs. Fields now," Alex said as his attention was brought back to the gravel road heading to the hangar. A battered sedan had turned onto the lane ahead of him.

Alex drove up to the open door of the hangar. Max had already moved the small floatplane out of the hangar and down to the dock. He was standing on his small pier beside the pressurized metal ramp he had in place. Alex remembered when Max had first shown him that ramp. Because its small platform lowered automatically, he could carry heavier loads of freight on his plane. If they had been able to go back to the clinic, Max could have even gotten a gurney on his plane. That would make Timmy more comfortable, but they didn't have time.

Max had his hand outstretched by the time Alex stepped out of his Jeep.

"You made good time," the pilot said as they shook hands.

Alex nodded. "It'll just take me a minute to carry the boy on. His mother is coming down your road, and my nurse will be going with us."

Max smiled in delight. "Maryann?"

Alex glared at the man. A dark-haired Irishman with a wicked sense of humor, Max was one of Treasure Creek's most noted bachelors. "Yeah."

"Magnificent," Max said as he started to walk toward the passenger side of the Jeep.

"I'll just go give her a hand. Maryann's an Irish name, isn't it?"

"Not a chance," Alex said as he matched his steps to the pilot's. He wasn't sure whether he was referring to Maryann's name or the unspoken inference about the likelihood of her dating the Irishman. Alex knew the man's reputation, and it had only been confirmed when he stayed in Alex's house one time. "Besides, she's religious."

Alex figured that would give the man pause. From all he had heard, the Irishman liked women who were easy on the eye and had no opinions about right and wrong, especially none that would interfere with his plans.

Max stopped and looked at Alex. "My mom, bless her dear departed soul, always wanted me to marry a religious woman."

"You're not thinking of marriage!" Alex stopped in astonishment.

The Irishman shrugged and gave another grin.

"We've got a serious situation here," Alex said curtly. "Leave my nurse alone."

With that, he finished walking to the Jeep and opened the back door. Maryann had gathered the blankets around Timmy and had him ready to be carried. Alex lifted the boy up, not realizing until he was heading toward the plane that he had left Max to help Maryann.

He heard the man's laugh and Maryann's answering chuckle.

Alex turned to look over his shoulder. The man was holding Maryann's elbow like she was fine china and might slip on the perfectly dry dirt.

"Hey, Max," Alex called. "I'll need you to help with the ramp."

He waited until he saw the other man make a gallant bow over Maryann's hand and kiss it goodbye. That's all Alex needed— a Sir Galahad to pilot the plane. The look of pure delight on Maryann's face didn't sit too well with him either. She probably didn't realize that anyone could go around kissing women's hands. It took a real man to carry the blankets.

"I'm here," Max said as he ran up to Alex and gave him a pat on the back. "Let me be sure that ramp is lined up. Too bad we don't have the boy in a wheelchair. I could lift him right up to the plane door with this thing."

"Maybe we'll need it on the way home," Alex said. He looked down at Timmy. The boy's face was white and he was shivering.

Alex heard a car park behind him and the sounds of Maryann talking to Mrs. Fields. He didn't have time to turn and greet the other woman though. He needed to get Timmy on the plane and ready for takeoff.

Maryann had her arm around Mrs. Fields and was urging her toward the plane. The wind was continuing to blow, so they bent into it a little as they hurried. The other woman was scared so Maryann said the only thing she could. "Dr. Havens is a good doctor. Timmy will have the best care possible. And it's only forty-five—maybe fifty—minutes to Juneau. When we're in the air, we'll call the hospital and they'll have an ambulance waiting for us when we land. "

Mrs. Fields nodded. "We should have taken Timmy back to the clinic yesterday, when he wanted us to. He must have known something was wrong inside."

Mrs. Fields stumbled slightly. The ground was rutted in one spot from the last rain.

"Careful." Maryann guided the other woman the rest of the way over the rough ground. Right then, there was no reason to bring up why Timmy wanted to go back to the clinic. There would be time enough to talk about the treasure map when Timmy was better.

Before anyone could say more, they were

climbing inside the small plane. After being in the wind, the inside of the plane seemed very quiet. Alex had settled Timmy across two of the backseats and managed to use the seat belts to be sure he stayed safe.

"Someone will need to sit in the copilot seat," Max said as he boarded. He paused in the passenger area before turning to the small opening leading to the cockpit. "This Cessna only carries four back there—and the boy is taking two places already."

Maryann looked around. Alex clearly needed to stay with Timmy. And Mrs. Fields was looking at her son like she wouldn't easily let him out of her sight.

"I'll sit there," Maryann said, even though she wasn't sure she wanted the view out of the copilot's seat. Heights made her nervous and the windows allowed one to see so much more from the cockpit than from the back of the plane.

"Perfect," Max said from where he sat in the pilot seat. "Everyone get buckled in and we'll be out of here."

Maryann had heard about float planes, so she wasn't surprised when Max started the engines and then taxied across the water leading out to the ocean. She barely had time to grab the sides of her seat before she felt the small plane lifting up.

"You can relax now," Max said quietly from the pilot's seat.

Maryann forced herself to let go of the seat. "I'm just a little nervous."

"Maybe you should try praying," the pilot said.

Maryann looked at him to see if he was teasing her. She supposed the Bible in her pocket did stand out. "Maybe I should. Especially because…"

She craned her neck to look behind her. Timmy's face was white, but the boy managed to smile back at her.

She turned around and Max nodded. "My mother would be praying if she were here with us. She was a woman of deep faith." He paused. "I miss her."

"I'm sure you do," Maryann said, suddenly full of sympathy. She had misjudged the man, thinking he was trying to see how far he could get with her, when all the time he was only remembering his poor mother.

"Do you have any brothers or sisters?" Maryann asked. She had glimpsed out of the window and preferred to keep her eyes focused inside. The rush of the climb for altitude was behind them, but the ground still looked a long way down.

"I've a sister in Seattle," Max said. "She comes up to visit me now and again. Next time she does, I'll be sure and introduce the two of you. I think you'd hit it off."

"I'd like that," Maryann said as she turned to look behind her. The noise of the plane meant she couldn't hear Alex or Mrs. Fields in the back, but she could see them sitting there. Timmy had his eyes closed, but Mrs. Fields managed to give a small wave to her, and Alex frowned at her for some reason. She smiled at them both.

When she straightened in her seat, Max had turned the plane slightly so they had a view of Mount McKinley in the distance. Wisps of clouds gathered around the snow-covered slopes of the mountain.

"It's beautiful," she breathed. The base of the mountain was covered with green pines, and the sun shining on the snow higher up made it look like the clouds and the mountain were merged into one. She had no idea there was so much verdant green in Alaska. From a distance, the trees looked like deep forest velvet, at least those at the lower regions of the mountains. Further up it was all shale and snow, with only slight traces of green here and there.

"Twenty thousand, three hundred and twenty feet above sea level," Max said, with pride in his voice. "They don't make them like Mount McKinley in the lower forty-eight. The natives call it The Big One."

Max turned the plane back to his original direction and continued, "I always like to pay my respects to The Big One when I set out on a flight. When you see her up in the sky like this, it's like she's there just for you. Someday I'm going to climb her. The north slope, I think."

"You'd remember it all your life if you did," Maryann said. Only now could she imagine the view from the top of the mountain. "It'd be something to tell your grandchildren."

Neither one of them spoke for a moment. The sound of the plane engine filled the air.

"So you're interested in having children, are you?" Max said with a sideways glance at her. "I mean, when the time comes and all?"

"Me?" Maryann hesitated. Not many men casually asked women that question. Then she realized he was probably asking because she was a nurse. "I love taking care of children. It's hard, of course, when they are as sick as Timmy."

She glanced back again. Mrs. Fields had her hand on Timmy's forehead, and Alex was leaning over him, too.

"Is he okay?" she asked loudly. The plane was noisy, but Alex managed to hear her anyway, and gave her a reassuring nod.

When she turned around they were no longer facing Mount McKinley. The view had changed to a series of smaller mountains and deep valleys. What wasn't covered with trees was gray shale.

"My sister says her kids scare years off her life," Max said with feeling. "But when a man gets as old as me—well, ask the doc back there, he's the same age—we start to think about getting married and raising a family."

"I wouldn't ask the doctor," Maryann said with a friendly smile. "He won't be marrying anytime soon. He's apparently got things to do before he even dates anyone."

"Really?" Max looked over at her in surprise. "He sure has me fooled, then."

"Well, it's true," Maryann said with more emphasis than was necessary. She needed to remember that herself. She more than anyone should know the pain that came from not facing reality in romance. Her parents had taught her that, if nothing else.

"Then he wouldn't mind if I ask you out sometime?" Max glanced over at her.

"Of course not," Maryann said just as firmly. It was none of Alex's business who she dated. Then she realized what she had said. "Not that—I mean, I haven't really had much time to go out since I've been in Treasure Creek."

"I see you going to church," Max said, his eyes straight ahead this time.

"Well, yes."

"A man like me doesn't always know what to do on a Sunday morning. Lately I've gone fishing early, and sometimes I sit in front of the General Store while the Olson twins dig worms for me out of their mother's rose garden. I've seen you walk out of Lizbet's in that pink dress you wear. It reminds me of—"

Maryann interrupted with a quick grin. "I know, it reminds you of your mother."

Max gave a rueful chuckle. "If I was to come to church some Sunday, would you let me sit with you? It's hard to sit down alone in a place like that."

Maryann nodded. "Everyone is welcome in church."

She thought for a moment and then added, "In fact, you can come Thursday night and sing carols with us. Amy is going to start us practicing for the Christmas pageant. You'll want to be part of that."

"Ah, the Christmas pageant. I might just do that. It's been a long time since I've used my fine Irish voice for singing. The ladies always comment on how they like that."

Max must have been content with that, she thought, because they spent the rest of the trip in silence. She gradually relaxed enough that she could lean forward so she could see more of the scenery as they passed over the mountainous area.

Maryann saw the airport at Juneau before she expected.

"I want to thank you for bringing us here," Maryann said. It seemed as though Timmy had done fine on the short flight. At least, no one had said anything, except to ask Max midflight to call for an ambulance to meet them.

"I was coming this way anyway." Max kept his attention on his instrument panel. "I have a passenger that needs to be picked up. The man said he's planning to surprise his brother."

"Oh," Maryann said, thinking maybe… and then dismissing her thought. "Did he say who?"

"The brother?" Max looked up briefly. "No, I didn't ask."

"What about the man who's coming? Did you get his name," Maryann persisted, but it was too late. Max had gotten his call back from the control tower and he was taking the plane down lower. The noise of the engines increased. She expected him to head for the runways by the low, flat terminal building, but instead he was aiming for the wooden structures along the edge of the ocean.

"It's the dock for floatplanes," Max said.

She gripped the edge of the seat again. This time she remembered to pray at the same time, though. She glanced behind her to see that everyone was ready to land. Then she began to recite the Twenty-third Psalm. She was still reciting it, her lips moving almost silently, when Max shut the engines off. The sudden drop in noise made her look up.

"Smooth as rocking a baby to sleep," Max said proudly. "Bet you didn't even feel the landing. Not on water like this."

"It *was* smooth," Maryann agreed.

"Thank you," Max said with a grin. "They'll be out with some kind of a ramp for us any minute now. They know we have a special circumstance, so they'll bring the best they have."

The airport at Juneau was backed by green mountains, most of them with splotches of snow near their tops. Other than that, the buildings were wood frame and looked a lot like those in Treasure Creek, except for the fact that there were more onion roofs.

Suddenly, Maryann heard a siren approaching.

"That'll be the ambulance we called," Max said as he turned around to look into the back. "How's everyone doing back there?"

No one had a chance to answer him, because the airport crew was there with the ramp and so was the ambulance. It didn't seem possible that more people could fit in the plane, but a couple of the paramedics managed to squeeze inside so they could decide how to best carry Timmy out to the ambulance.

Maryann was permitted to ride in the back of the ambulance with Alex and one of the paramedics. Mrs. Fields rode in the front with the driver. The first thing the paramedics did was to wrap the blankets back around Timmy. Maryann couldn't get a good look at the boy, not with the paramedic, and then Alex, tending him so closely.

She knew he couldn't be in better hands, though. Alex might be The Ice Man in some ways, but he didn't give up on his patients.

He'd pull Timmy through with the sheer force of his determination. He might be leaving Alaska in a few weeks, but he would do his duty by everyone until then. She had no doubt of that. Even as she watched Alex, he lifted his head and looked straight at her. She could see in his eyes that he was very worried. So she smiled at him.

In a moment, his whole face lightened and he nodded back. They really were a good team, Maryann told herself. She only wished that realization made her happy.

Chapter Seven

Once at the hospital, Maryann helped Mrs. Fields get Timmy registered, so he could be transferred to a regular room. Alex had been obviously reluctant for them to go, but he couldn't leave Timmy in the curtained-off cot where he was lying, and a nurse had just come over to explain that someone needed to fill out paperwork.

"So he's in emergency now?" the young woman behind the counter asked as she frowned at a computer screen. She didn't look more than twenty years old. "I don't see him listed here."

Maryann and Timmy's mother were standing side-by-side at the counter. Maryann had her nurse's uniform on, and she had been hoping it would help ease things along. So far the clerk had barely looked at it.

"We just brought him in," Maryann said in her most professional voice when Mrs. Fields didn't speak. "Timothy Fields. Pediatric. He came in by ambulance with Dr. Havens from Treasure Creek about twenty minutes ago. The boy doesn't have a room yet."

The clerk looked up. She wore gold-framed glasses and had her hair pulled back in a French braid of some sort. Her eyelashes sparkled. "Do you know which of our doctors here in the hospital is handling him?"

"I could go back and ask. The boy's got pneumonia and some complications—"

"That would be Doctor Stuart, then," the clerk said as she looked back at the computer screen and punched in some letters. "Ah, here I see it. Now, your question is?"

"We want to see about getting my son set up with a room in the hospital," Mrs. Fields said softly. She had her clasped hands resting on top of the counter. Maryann figured she was the only one who noticed how white the woman's knuckles were when she spoke. "He's in the emergency room, but—"

"It says here he's stabilizing," the clerk said as she read the computer screen. "Dr. Stuart indicated it's not required that he stay past the time in the emergency room."

"But that's not right," Maryann gasped.

"Alex—I mean, Dr. Havens—said Timmy needs to be monitored closely. He's sick and—"

The clerk looked up from her computer. "Is Dr. Havens on staff here?"

"No, I don't think so," Maryann said. "But—"

"Of course, you can choose to admit the boy," the woman said with a smile. "Perhaps your insurance company will agree with your doctor and authorize him to stay."

Maryann's heart sank as she exchanged a glance with Timmy's mother.

"I'm afraid we don't have any insurance right now," Mrs. Fields admitted quietly. Maryann watched as she pressed her hands together more tightly.

"We can make payments, though." She took a deep breath and continued. "I have some pay stubs with me. You can deduct the payments if you want from my checks. And then we have our Permanent Fund checks coming. My husband and I are good for the money. We just need some time."

The clerk let Timmy's mother finish before answering. "I'm truly sorry. If you don't have insurance, we need prepayment of at least fifty percent of the expected total. In cash or credit card. That's hospital policy for optional admissions."

No one spoke for a moment.

"How much would that be?" Maryann finally asked the young woman. "The amount you would need for the prepayment? For this kind of illness?"

The clerk studied her computer screen before she looked up and spoke. "I'd guess we'd need eight to ten thousand. That covers part of the room, the tests, some of the doctor charges. If you don't have the cash, we do take a credit card."

Maryann put her hand on the middle of Mrs. Fields's back. She was worried the woman might faint. The young clerk hadn't sounded unkind, but there was no way Mrs. Fields had that kind of money. Not even tucked away in a bank account someplace. With her husband out of work and four little children, the household probably couldn't even pay all its regular bills.

Mrs. Fields shook her head, biting her lower lip at the same time. She was on the verge of tears. "What do we do? Is there someone we can talk to? Something we can sign? I suppose we could sign over the title to our car, but it's ten years old, so I don't know that it would do any good. And the pickup is practically worthless. We'll give you whatever you want, though. He's just a little boy."

The clerk concentrated on the computer screen, even though Maryann doubted there was anything new to be seen. Finally she said, "I'll get my supervisor. I don't think there's anything she can do, but, perhaps she can speak with Dr. Stuart. If he says it's necessary for Timmy to stay we have to admit him."

"Yes," Maryann said, nodding. Surely there had to be some provision for people without money. "We'll talk to her."

The young woman dialed a number on her telephone and spoke quietly into the mouthpiece. When she hung up the phone, she looked up and said. "It'll be a couple of minutes. Mrs. Haynes is in a meeting, but it's almost finished. You can wait over there."

The clerk gestured to a row of padded chairs on the far wall. Each chair was connected to the other by a black metal bar, but the chairs themselves looked comfortable. Maryann guided Mrs. Fields to where they could sit down.

"I'm sure they have many situations like this," Maryann said firmly when they had both seated themselves on the gray vinyl chairs. A framed print of Mount McKinley hung on the wall behind their chairs, a bald eagle flying across the corner of the picture. "This Mrs. Haynes will know what to do."

Mrs. Fields nodded. "You're right. Other people must be in our situation. I don't even know this Dr. Stuart. It shouldn't be his opinion that prevents Timmy from staying. What if he's wrong?"

Maryann put her hand over the other woman's and leaned closer. "The important thing is that Timmy is here now. Maybe Dr. Stuart hadn't had a chance to examine him yet."

It was the only hope Maryann could offer, although she wondered how the hospital could let the man make that kind of decision without looking at the patient. If the doctor had gone to see Timmy, though, Alex would have convinced him the boy needed to be admitted. She had seen him stand up for his patients before, and he was fearless. If he thought Timmy needed to be in a room in this hospital, he would make it happen if he had to take it up with the hospital board of directors.

She wished Alex was here with her now; he'd know what to do.

"I'm going to get Dr. Havens," Maryann said suddenly to Mrs. Fields as she stood. "I'll be right back."

Maryann quickly followed the blue line back to the emergency room and spoke briefly with the nurse at the admitting desk there. They each remembered the other from when Timmy had been brought in, so Maryann was on her way in no time.

She checked the room numbers until she found the one the nurse had given her. There were several curtained-off areas in the room, but Timmy at least had a proper hospital bed. She hesitated at the door. Timmy was in the middle bed. Alex was standing at the foot of the boy's bed and he was talking in a low voice with another doctor. Alex had a chart in his hand that could only belong to Timmy.

"Excuse me," Maryann said as she walked to where she could see Timmy. The boy was lying so still in his bed that she glanced over at the monitor to reassure herself that he was breathing. She knew the little red lights would be flashing and a beep would be sounding if anything was wrong.

Alex turned and she felt a shiver of awareness go down her body. He was rumpled; his shirt collar was crooked and he'd been running his fingers through his hair. The lines in his face were more pronounced than she'd ever noticed before. His eye sockets were deeper and his jaw less relaxed. But the intensity on his face took her breath away. He might not be the most handsome man in the world right now, but he was her hero. He was already fighting for Timmy, she could see it in the steel of his eyes.

Alex said something to the other doctor before he walked back to the doorway with her.

"How's his mother doing?" Alex asked when he got close. He leaned against the doorjamb slightly and his back gave them some privacy from the doctor in the room. He hunched a little forward, as though he were creating a space for just the two of them. She had to mentally pull herself away. She couldn't take gestures like that personally, not when he was going away so soon.

"We're having a bit of trouble admitting Timmy," Maryann said, her voice low. She wasn't looking up at Alex. "Dr. Stuart says he doesn't need to stay—that he's stabilized. I don't even know this Dr. Stuart. What are we going to do?"

Then she felt Alex's fingers on her chin, tilting her head up.

"I know you're worried," he said softly, looking into her eyes. "I'm sorry I wasn't out there with you. We'll find a way. Trust me. I'm talking to Dr. Stuart now."

Maryann could only stare at him. She knew he was treating her like a patient, using that calm, steady "trust me" voice. But at this point, she almost didn't care.

"I was hoping you were," she finally said, not bothering to hide her relief. "I figure he just hasn't examined Timmy yet."

"He's seeing him," Alex said with a tight smile. "We just have a difference of opinion."

Maryann smiled. "Well, you'll just change his mind then."

Alex watched the stress drain out of Maryann's face. He was amazed and humbled that she had so much confidence in him, especially when he didn't know how he was going to get Timmy admitted as a regular patient here. Dr, Stuart had just been saying that the hospital was taking a hard line these days on noninsurance admissions that were discretionary. They had too many old, outstanding bills that would never be paid. It would be a fight to get Timmy admitted if Dr. Stuart didn't say it was absolutely necessary.

"I'll come talk to you when I get a chance," Alex said, giving Maryann his best shot at a smile. She really was a trouper. She hadn't even berated him for his poor behavior last night, and he wasn't sure when he'd get a chance to explain himself to her—or to sit down and figure out his reaction for himself. "I'll be right out."

"Just follow the blue line," Maryann said as she turned to leave. "Mrs. Fields and I will be waiting in admissions."

He watched her as she walked away.

"Friend of the family?" Dr. Stuart asked when Alex walked back.

"My nurse," he answered, wondering if he should add something more. That certainly wasn't an adequate description, but he doubted Dr. Stuart wanted to know the confusion he felt around Maryann these days. "Now, where were we."

"You were showing me that X-ray."

Fifteen minutes later, Dr. Stuart was paged and said he had to leave to see another patient. Alex suspected Dr. Stuart knew he was walking a thin line, but he was unwilling to authorize hospital admittance for Timmy. His parting shot to Alex had been, "If you're so sure the boy needs to stay, you find the money to make it happen."

Alex walked back to Timmy's bed. A nurse had just taken the boy's vital signs and he did seem better. Alex knew the improvement gave false hope, though. He'd treated Timmy through enough illnesses to know how the boy handled sickness. He'd fight it off and look as if he was winning, but then he'd crash.

"How's it going?" Alex asked, bending down.

The boy looked up at him and made the effort to smile. "When can I go home?"

If they took Timmy to Treasure Creek, they might not have enough time to get him back to the hospital when he became worse. Alex refused to risk it.

"Not until you're well," Alex promised him.

With that, Alex left and started walking down the hallway to the office, his eyes on that blue line as he thought about what he'd say to the woman who handled the admissions.

"Excuse me," a man's voice said.

Alex looked up from his thoughts. An orderly was standing there with an empty gurney.

"Oh, I'm sorry," Alex said as he stepped to the side of the hallway. He'd blocked the man's way. He should know better. The corridors of a hospital were busier than some major freeways at rush hour. He'd forgotten how fast-paced things were. Down in Los Angeles, it would be even more frantic. He hadn't realized how accustomed he'd become to the pace in Treasure Creek, where he had time to stop and think about something that wasn't related to his patients. He even regularly took a short lunch break. Of course, there had been more fast-paced moments his first year there, but now he was able to do so much to prevent problems with his patients that his days usually went like clockwork.

He looked around. The astringent smell was all too familiar. As was the flash of the nurse-call buttons over the patients doors. Then there was the sound of the metal cart rolling down the hall, signaling lunch for the patients. Adrenaline used to course through him when he was in a hospital as an intern. He had charged into medicine like he could bend the outcomes for the sick to his will. He knew better now, although he still, all too often, felt like he was the only advocate some of his smallest patients had.

Alex straightened his shoulders. Ironically, if Timmy was a gunshot or stabbing victim, he stood a better chance of getting a room without qualifying financially.

He followed the blue line to admissions, taking long strides. He was going to justify Maryann's faith in him. He'd find a way to pull this off.

He turned the corner into the admissions area and saw a trim, dark-haired woman in a tailored suit walking toward Maryann and Mrs. Fields. She must be the admissions supervisor. She looked professional, right down to the high heels on her feet.

Alex took a moment to smooth back his hair and straighten his shirt collar. He wished he'd worn his oxfords instead of his sports shoes, but he'd hardly taken his dress shoes out of the closet since he'd been in Alaska.

"Dr. Havens," Maryann greeted him formally as he approached them. "Come meet Mrs. Haynes."

"Pleased to meet you," Alex said as he held his hand out to the woman. "You have a fine hospital. Worked here long?"

He guessed she'd come to Alaska recently, because of her heels, but he hoped not. Someone who had heard enough of the hardship stories around here might have more compassion.

She took his hand and inclined her head to him. "Not long. I used to work in Los Angeles. The Huntington Hospital."

Alex's heart sank, but he didn't stop to examine why. An expensive hospital in a well-to-do area had nothing in common with these small towns in Alaska that struggled to survive.

"I've heard good things about the place," Alex said. And he had.

"Thank you, Doctor. I was very proud to work there. Now, I understand you have a patient you want to admit." She paused and raised an eyebrow. "Without insurance."

Alex wondered if his clothes were more rumpled than he thought.

"I was hoping we could talk about that, yes," he said and forced himself to give a smile as close as possible to the one Max would be dishing out.

Mrs. Haynes did seem to relax more. "You must understand, we only accept true emergencies without insurance or a cash deposit. Perhaps the family could qualify for a loan from a local bank?"

Alex glanced down and saw the color drain from Mrs. Fields's face. He doubted there was much hope of a bank loan in the family's future.

"Mrs. Fields?" he asked gently.

She shook her head.

"I don't suppose the boy has any Native American heritage?" Mrs. Haynes asked. "We do have funds to accommodate those with enough Native American blood to qualify for them. I don't know the exact tribes off the top of my head, but I know it's generally one-sixteenth that they're looking for."

He saw Mrs. Fields start to wring her hands. She shook her head when he glanced over at her.

"I'm afraid not. But certainly, there has to be some grant money or something," Alex said. This was a hospital. They were supposed to heal people.

"I'm sorry," Mrs. Haynes said. She gave one of those business smiles. "He does have the eight hours in the emergency room. Our Dr. Stuart feels the boy will be well enough to go home after that."

Alex started to protest that eight hours wasn't enough, when he looked down at Timmy's mother. She was practically in tears.

He turned to Maryann. "Maybe you could take Mrs. Fields to the cafeteria and get her some soup of something. It's been a long time since any of us had breakfast."

Maryann nodded and stood. She looked tired, too.

"I'll stay and figure this out," Alex said once both women were standing. He'd already realized that there was only one way to end this standoff with the hospital, and he didn't want either of the women to be around to witness his actions.

"Perhaps we can go to your office," Alex said when he was alone with Mrs. Haynes.

They walked down a tiled hallway and stopped at an office with a window overlooking the front lawn of the building. Her office was, of course, depressingly neat. Maybe she hadn't been there long enough to have a full in-box. She did have a rather large fern on her filing cabinet though, which encouraged him since they were hard to grow and that meant she must be giving it good care.

"Please, be seated." Mrs. Haynes gestured to the office chair sitting in front of her desk as she sat. "I find that these discussions about money always make me wish I'd taken time to eat a better breakfast before leaving for work."

Alex chuckled politely.

"You're sure the parents don't have some stock certificates their great-grandfather left them?" she asked when they were both seated. "Maybe a fishing boat they can sell?"

Alex shook his head. "I've been to their place several times over the past few years. They are who they appear to be. Hardworking for the most part, but down on their luck. Four kids, a couple of vehicles that barely run. Mrs. Fields works at one of the hotels in town, cleaning rooms. Even with tips, she doesn't make enough to keep the family in food and clothes. At least not all year round. She probably made enough to feed them this summer, but now that tourist season is coming to a close, she won't be seeing the same tips and will probably have her hours cut."

Alex felt discouraged listing the family's problems.

Mrs. Haynes was thoughtful for a moment. Then she asked, "You're sure they don't have any Native American blood? Maybe a great-grandfather or something?"

Alex shook his head. "The couple said once that all four of their parents were from Europe. They met in Seattle and moved up here ten years ago."

"Well, then..."

Neither one of them moved.

"If Timmy can only stay the eight-hour max—and we take him out of the emergency room after that—can we readmit him for another eight?" Alex asked finally.

Mrs. Haynes smiled but shook her head. "Afraid not. Rules."

Alex took a deep breath. There was no other way. Not that he could see. "Could you give me a total of what is needed for the deposit?"

She nodded and turned to the computer that was at the side of her desk.

Alex closed his eyes. He told himself he wasn't praying, he was thinking. If God happened to listen in, Alex had no problem with that. He could use some good advice.

He didn't know how to stretch what he had, not with all he needed to do. He'd saved every penny he'd made giving those tours for Alaska's Treasures over the three years he'd been up here. That included every tip he'd been given, even the small ones. He received enough in his monthly salary to pay for his needs and his brother's attendant. The total in his savings account was $20,456.22. He needed twenty thousand for the down payment on the construction costs. In order for the bank to give him a loan for the rest. The bank wouldn't go any lower than that. He'd asked the last time he was down in Los Angeles.

Alex couldn't stand by and do nothing. He hadn't been able to act to save his brother all those years ago, but he could do something now. He didn't know when he'd be able to replace the money from his savings, but he'd be alive to do it. Which was more than Timmy might be.

Mrs. Haynes cleared her throat. Alex opened his eyes and looked up.

"We'd need eight thousand six hundred dollars up front," the woman said, and lifted a hand to stall any protests. "That's already giving him every discount I can and some I shouldn't."

Alex nodded. "Do you take American Express?"

He pulled his card out, grateful that his occupation qualified him for their gold.

Mrs. Haynes nodded uncertainly as she eyed the card. "Is that from your clinic? Or The City of Treasure Creek?"

He shook his head. "No, it's my personal card." He held it up. "Alex Havens."

The woman leaned across her desk and took the card. "I see. I assume they'll pay you back then."

Alex grunted. The woman could make any assumptions she wanted. He was under no such expectations, however. The Fields family would never be able to pay him back. They just didn't make enough. He'd just have to find a way to replace the money himself.

He smiled. Maybe he'd find another treasure map like the one Amy had. More than one of those old prospectors must have hid their gold. None of them trusted the banks and few of them had much faith in their friends, so a hole in the ground probably looked pretty good to them when they pondered where to put their treasure.

"I'll take this up to the front desk and have them run it for you," Mrs. Haynes said as she stood and pointed. "Help yourself to some chocolates in the bookcase over there."

Alex turned his head to look where she indicated. Sure enough, there was a cut-glass dish filled with foil-wrapped candy. He stood up and walked over to them. He recognized the brand name on the foil; these were quality sweets.

He put two in his pocket. Maybe later he could share one with Maryann. That is—he thought for a moment—he assumed she wasn't just talking to him as Dr. Havens. He hoped she was still talking to him when he was only Alex.

He paused for a second and then put another candy in his pocket. It never hurt to have some extra persuasion.

Chapter Eight

Looking through the hospital window, Maryann could see that the sky outside had started to turn dark. She was sitting quietly in a chair next to the window in Timmy's room. The boy was sleeping and breathing more evenly than he had been since he arrived. The nurses and doctors had been hovering over him for the past hour and had just left a while ago. She did not know how Dr. Havens had performed the miracle of getting the hospital to admit Timmy as a regular patient, but she was grateful that he had.

She no sooner thought of the man than he silently walked into the room. He'd been working with the other doctors and nurses earlier, while she'd been sitting with Mrs. Fields. Ordinarily, she'd want to be closer to the action, but she knew how lonely it could get for someone in those big hospital waiting rooms, and Mrs. Fields did not look strong.

"Did Max pick her up?" Maryann whispered softly so she wouldn't disturb Timmy. Alex had taken Mrs. Fields down to the hospital entrance so she could join Max in the cab when he came by. She was flying back to Treasure Creek with him tonight, and then coming back tomorrow morning, when the pilot made another trip down to Juneau.

Alex nodded as he pulled a metal folding chair closer to where she sat. Quietly, he said, "I was afraid she wouldn't sleep if she stayed here. And she already looked ready to collapse."

Maryann nodded and kept her voice low. "She was probably worried about what to tell the other children, too. Not to mention her husband."

She scooted her chair closer to the window so Alex's would fit in better.

When he put his chair down, she said, "That was nice of Max to have his cab come by and get Mrs. Fields. I don't think she's ever taken a cab."

"He's a prince, all right," Alex muttered as he sat down in the chair. He reached into his pocket and pulled out a foil-wrapped piece of candy. "Want one?"

"Sure." Maryann took the candy from his open hand. "This didn't come from the vending machine, did it? I didn't see it there."

Alex shook his head in disgust. "There's nothing in that machine that even resembles chocolate. Which is shortsighted, if you ask me. No one wants vitamin drinks when they're waiting around here."

Maryann unwrapped the candy and put it in her mouth.

"Humm," she said as she closed her eyes. "That's delicious."

"Does that make me a prince, too, then?" Alex whispered, his voice low and teasing.

Maryann opened her eyes and shook her head. She was glad to see he was smiling, instead of looking as grim as he'd been.

"You're not a prince," she informed him quietly. "You're the king."

Alex raised his eyebrow. "You mean the grand pooh-bah?"

She nodded her head and licked the last of the chocolate off her lips. "That's exactly who I mean. Anyone who gives out chocolate like that deserves a good title."

Alex felt his whole body go on alert. His heart was tottering on some brink, and he couldn't afford for it to go tumbling over, no matter how pink her cheeks got when she

struggled not to laugh. He'd just postponed
the date at which he would have that clinic in
Los Angeles up and operating. He wouldn't be
a free man until he'd put the money back into
his savings account and managed to build that
clinic. It could take years, and he couldn't ask
someone to wait for him that long—certainly
not someone as full of life as Maryann.

"Ever been to Southern California?" he
heard his voice ask, even though his head was
wondering what he was doing. "You know—
Hollywood, surfers, the beach?"

"Do you like the beach?" she asked with a
new light in her eyes.

"I can handle the beach," he answered,
thinking he'd have to get that old umbrella out
of his parents' garage. It was probably falling
apart by now, but it might look charming. He
hoped she didn't expect him to surf. "Malibu
or Santa Monica are both great."

She nodded. "One of the fancy women
wanted to know if you liked the beach. I think
she might be the best one of the bunch. Maybe
I should introduce you."

"Maybe you should," he said, just to show
that her words didn't sting. "At least she might
not prefer Irish men to me."

Maryann looked up at him in surprise and
asked, "What do you mean?"

Then she suddenly sat up straighter. "Max said you were ready to start dating someone. I told him he was wrong and that you weren't, because you sure hadn't seemed—"

Maryann stopped and closed her mouth tight. Then she crossed her arms.

Alex couldn't tell whether to give her a hug or some space, so he reached into his pocket again. "Another chocolate?"

At least that made her look at him.

"I didn't quite realize you were asking me if *I* liked the beach," she finally admitted. "I don't really know, I've never been in a beach community. I know we're close to the ocean here, but no one can really claim it's part of a beach area. People seem to refer to it mostly as 'the coast.' And with the water being so cold, no one goes swimming, even in the summer. And no one ever suns themselves. I mean it's hard to think of it as the beach and—"

Her voice was starting to break up, so he lifted the chocolate higher in his hand.

"I think the green wrapper means it's mint," he whispered. Her face flushed and he wasn't sure quite what that meant. He reached over and brushed her cheek with the back of his hand. He still held the chocolate. "Warm enough in here?"

The light was dim and the shadows hid

her eyes. She was silent for a moment and then she nodded. "It's fine. I was just a little confused," she said, and he held his breath. Maybe she was feeling some of the stirring he felt. "The other candy was mint, too, and it was a blue wrapper."

"Well, I guess it's not a perfect system, then," he said. Which had to be the understatement of the year. He was down two pieces of chocolate, and he still hadn't figured out whether it would be okay to ask her out.

"I could do some per diem work when I get back to L.A.," he said, thinking it couldn't take that long to earn another seventeen thousand. Maybe he was only putting himself behind six months or so.

"Any hospital would be fortunate to have you," she said. But he noticed her shoulders had stiffened as she sat there. And she wasn't looking at him now. He wasn't talking work with her—he was talking their future. But he could see where she wouldn't understand that.

He felt a catch in his throat. The moment was going to pass him by.

"So, do you want to go to the beach with me sometime?" he asked, his voice coming out a little hoarse and raspy. He resisted the urge to clear his throat.

"Around here?" she asked, her eyebrow rising in astonishment.

He realized he couldn't very well invite her to Los Angeles; he wasn't even there himself. "Sure. It'd be fun."

"Okay," she said, and then swallowed. "But we'd have to go to church first."

"Why?"

"That way, we'd be friends."

"But we're friends now, I hope. I—" And then it hit him. "Max already invited you to go to the beach with him, didn't he?"

Alex felt his jaw tense. That would be just like his pilot friend. He'd lure a woman down to that dock of his and put a candle on a blanket and spin her some yarn about it being the beach. Then he'd snuggle with her until she didn't care if they were sitting on some sand or an iceberg.

Maryann shook her head. "No, he asked if he could come to church with me."

Of course, Alex thought to himself, the man was more devious than even he had given him credit for. The beach was nothing compared to sitting in a pew with a woman like Maryann. "*I'm* free this Sunday."

"Don't forget Thursday, when we rehearse for the pageant," Maryann said with a tiny smile on her lips.

"I'll be there on Thursday, and on Sunday as well," Alex said decisively.

"Really?" She seemed surprised.

"And Sunday dinner afterwards," he said firmly.

Maryann nodded. "That would be nice."

There was a slight moan from the hospital bed and Alex went over and put his hand on Timmy's forehead. The boy was hooked up to the best machines in the hospital, Alex thought to himself, and it still seemed natural to read his temperature by touching his forehead. He hadn't always been that kind of a doctor. He'd learned a lot by tending to the children of Treasure Creek. It wasn't always about the exact number of the temperature. Sometimes people just wanted to feel someone's hand on their head when they were sick.

Alex turned to look at Maryann. "He's fine. I'd like to eat dinner together, but I think one of us should be here in case he wakes up. We'll be here all night. So if you want to take the first meal shift, I'll go eat when you come back."

Maryann stood and reached in her pocket. She pulled out that Bible she'd been carrying around. "If he wakes up, could you read him the Twenty-third Psalm. I told his father I would and—"

Alex swallowed. "Sure. I could do that."

"I've marked the place with the blue candy wrapper," she said as she handed him the white Bible. "The print's kind of small, so you'll have to sit in the light when you read it."

Alex smiled. He'd already promised to go to church with her and to the rehearsal for the Christmas pageant. He should have known she'd have him reading a psalm or two next.

"Have a nice dinner," he said as she left the room.

Maryann decided she needed to do something before she went to the hospital cafeteria. She needed to call her cousin, so she went down to the hospital entrance and walked outside to use her cell phone. The night was early, but the temperature had dropped significantly when the sun went down. She huddled between the glass doors to the hospital and a side column.

"Karenna?" she asked when someone answered on the other end of the phone.

"How are you? Amy dropped by to tell me you had flown to Juneau with Timmy Fields. That poor kid. Is he okay?" Karenna asked in a rush.

"Thankfully, yes," Maryann said. "Dr.

Havens moved heaven and earth to get him admitted, so he has a room and his breathing is better. Everyone is encouraged. They think another day or two will get him well enough that he can go home."

"Oh, good," her cousin said.

"I'm staying with him tonight though," Maryann added. "Dr. Havens is here, too, and…"

She was suddenly conscious of the heavy silence on the other end of the phone. By now, her cousin should be trying to talk over her.

"Karenna?"

"You're staying there with The Ice Man?" her cousin asked. She didn't sound very pleased. "He should have let you come home. Most employers don't require their workers to stay all night, especially when he's there to handle it."

"I thought you wanted me to get to know him?" Maryann countered. "Didn't you sit there the other night in the diner and say I needed to get to know The Ice Man before I judged him?"

"Well, yes," Karenna admitted. "But I didn't mean you should spend the night with him."

"We're in the hospital with hundreds of other people," Maryann protested.

"Oh, I didn't mean I was worried in that

way. I know you. Besides, your doctor would never—"

"He asked me out," Maryann interrupted. She might be stretching that a little, but it felt good to say it to her cousin, because—well, just because her cousin shouldn't be making assumptions.

The phone was silent for several seconds.

"Really?" Karenna finally asked. "He asked you out? Like on a date?"

"Yes, he did," Maryann said a little smugly. "He's coming to church with me and then he invited me to dinner. And then sometime, we're going to the beach."

"That's very nice," Karenna said, her voice sounding cautious. "But did he say it was a date?"

"It was implied."

"Because I'm wondering why he'd ask you out now, when he's leaving in a few weeks. Of course, it's still good. Don't get me wrong, but—"

"You think he's just being nice, don't you?" Maryann said. That thought had occurred to her, too. She hadn't really believed it, but maybe that's the way it was.

"No, not that—" Karenna was quiet for so long Maryann wondered if they'd been disconnected. And then she spoke. "It's just that Gage told me the guys had given your doctor a hard time at Lizbet's during his birthday dinner. I mean, at first, because of the fancy women. And then they noticed he seemed to be, well, putting his arm around you and everything, and they thought—well, they hoped it wasn't just—you know how guys are when they're being teased. Like their manhood is called into question. Gage thought they might have given him too hard a time and he was trying to prove something to them."

"Oh," Maryann said. Gage did have a point. The doctor had certainly acted different after that dinner than he had before it. Usually, she picked up on those kinds of things. And she was sure she would have figured it out eventually, if anything like that was happening. "Well, it probably won't come to anything anyway. He'll probably call to say he's sick on Sunday morning. Or tired. He could certainly claim to be exhausted. I would understand that, after the last few days."

"I could have Gage talk to him if you want," Karenna offered.

"Please, no," Maryann said. "That would be awkward. Remember, I have to work with the man for another…" She thought a moment. "Two and a half more weeks."

"But if you want to date someone," Karenna said, "I'm sure Gage can find someone for you. There are lots of single men around here."

"No, no. I wanted to get settled here before I started to date," Maryann said. "I still haven't unpacked all my boxes."

"That's smart," Karenna said. "You make sure the doctor doesn't work you too hard, either."

"I'm not working at all right now," Maryann said. "I'm on my way to the cafeteria to get something to eat."

"Be sure and stay away from the mashed potatoes," her cousin advised. "They're always instant. And the vegetables are usually overcooked."

"I'm sure I'll find something worth eating," Maryann said. Now that her cousin had ruined her fantasy of having a date, she didn't want her to ruin her dinner, too. However, Karenna did mean well, she told herself. "I'll call you when I get back home."

"Love you," Karenna said softly.

"Me, too," Maryann answered and meant it. Then they hung up.

Maryann realized she was shivering and she slipped her cell phone into her purse so she could hug herself for warmth as she walked back to the glass doors that opened into the hospital. The doors opened automatically and she was thankful for small favors. Until a person had put their cold hands on a freezing metal bar to open a door, they didn't truly appreciate the automatic ones.

Inside the hospital, she made her way to the cafeteria. She'd been there earlier with Mrs. Fields, and the vegetable soup had been tolerable and hot. She hadn't noticed what the posted menu listed as entrees for tonight, but she thought she smelled spaghetti as she walked down the hall to the dining area.

It didn't take her long to eat her plate of spaghetti and string beans. Then she poured herself a cup of decaf coffee and sat back down to sip it. She felt right at home in her nurse's uniform here, although she noticed there were more blue-and-green uniforms than white. She supposed she was just a traditional kind of a person.

When she finished her coffee, she stood up. She wondered if Timmy had woken up at all while she'd been gone. She stopped in the gift shop to buy a magazine on the way back through the lobby area, and saw that they had a few birthday cards. Most of them were for little kids, but there was one with a sailboat that simply said "Happy Birthday" inside. She bought it for Alex. She'd sign it "Your Nurse," but at least he'd have a card.

She walked down the hallway toward Timmy's room and wondered if she should have bought some of those red silk roses in the gift shop for the boy. They would have certainly brightened up the room.

Alex put a thumb on the page to keep his place. He was reading to Timmy, and the boy was altogether too alert.

"You ever been to The Valley of the Shadow of Death?" the boy asked. His voice wasn't firm, but it was clear. "Makes me think of Darth Vader—some creature that breathes like that." Timmy's eyes brightened. "Did I sound like that when I was breathing with this machine on? I think I could."

"Don't even try it," Alex said as he noticed his young charge trying to hold his breath so he could make the machine distort his breathing. "And I think the reference is an actual place."

"Like a valley of death? Like what? Like the north slope?" Timmy asked, puzzled.

"Well, I suppose in a way," Alex agreed. "It's a real place where people went back then."

"Humph. Like 'Hey there! Though I go through the north slope, I shall fear no evil'." The boy said, weighing his words. "Naw, that just doesn't sound right. No one goes through the north slope."

"Well, then think of a valley," Alex said, trying to curb his impatience. "Anyway, as I was saying, 'Yea, though I go through the Valley of Death, I shall—'"

"What's the name of the valley by Treasure Creek?" Timmy asked.

"I don't think it has a name," Alex said as he lay the Bible down on the bed. "Maybe it's time for you to take another nap."

"I am a little tired," Timmy admitted. "Can you tuck me in?"

"What?" Alex was already starting to stand up so he could turn the light off.

"My mom always tucks me in when it's time to go to sleep," Timmy admitted a little sheepishly.

"Oh, well," Alex stammered and then reached out and pulled on the covers so that they rested just under Timmy's chin. "There. Is that it?"

Timmy looked at him, clearly uncertain about whether to proceed.

"You can tell me," Alex said gently.

"She sometimes kisses my head," Timmy said. "Just for good sleeping."

Alex smiled. "Of course. I should have known."

He leaned over and kissed his patient on the forehead. "Sweet dreams."

Timmy nodded and closed his eyes. Alex figured he would be sound asleep within seconds, given the amount of medication he was taking.

He reached up and turned off the light near the bed. The overhead lights were off as well, so the only light was coming from a couple of plug-in lights along the wall. Of course, the door was open, and—he turned around and saw Maryann leaning on the doorjamb with a look of pure mischief on her face.

"What?" he said.

"I didn't know good-night kisses were something doctors were giving out now," she said softly as she stood there. "That was cute."

Alex leaned back in his chair. It was a rare treat to be sitting in a dark room and seeing Maryann backlit from the lights in the hallway. It gave golden tones to her brown hair and added shadows to her face that seemed to shift with her expression.

"Did you read to Timmy?" she asked as she walked into the room.

"Tried to," he said as he glanced over to where the Bible still sat on the bedcovers. "But not hard enough, I guess. We didn't make it through the whole psalm. He had questions about The Valley of the Shadow of Death."

Maryann nodded. "It was good to see him talking again."

"It would be better if he wasn't talking about death."

"I doubt it's because he's thinking he might die."

Alex nodded. He supposed that was true.

Maryann walked over to the bed and picked up the Bible. "Want to keep it for awhile?"

Alex shook his head. Reading that Bible had been hard for more reasons than that Timmy had been distracting. It was difficult for Alex to even pick it up, because he felt like he didn't deserve to read it. He'd been a Christian once, or at least he had gone to church as a child. And he'd given everything up, with no more thought than if he'd given up an old pair of sneakers. Something like that wouldn't be easy for God to forgive.

Maryann lifted the Bible into the light and looked at it closely. "The map's still here."

Alex shrugged. "Timmy hasn't mentioned it and neither have I."

"I wonder if he's forgotten," she said thoughtfully.

"I'm sure it will come back to him," Alex said. The promise of treasure seemed to take hold of people and not let go. Although, from all he could tell, Timmy hadn't wanted the fortune for himself, so maybe that made it less consuming.

Maryann sat down in the chair she'd used earlier, and Alex pulled his folding chair closer to her so he wouldn't disturb the boy.

"They have spaghetti for dinner," she said after a few moments. "It's not bad. It's even got some fresh mushrooms in it. And they serve it with garlic toast. Nice and crispy."

Alex nodded. He could sit here all night doing nothing, but he was hungry. And if this cafeteria was like all the other hospital cafeterias he'd eaten in, the food didn't improve as the night wore on. In fact, it often didn't even last that long. He'd best get down there.

"Timmy is going to be all right, isn't he?" Maryann asked quietly from the chair.

Alex nodded. The treatments had been working. By now even Dr. Stuart acknowledged how sick the boy had been. "He's over the worst of it."

Alex looked at Maryann. Her face was not turned toward him, but he could sense she was tired, so he added, "You don't need to worry."

Getting Timmy admitted to the hospital had saved the boy's life, but Alex didn't want Maryann to know how close it had been.

"That's good," she said. "I think I should go back to Treasure Creek tomorrow morning, when Max flies back. I could at least call and reschedule the clinic appointments, rather than ask someone else to do it."

Alex put his hand on her shoulder.

She looked up at him. "Timmy won't need someone sitting with him after tonight, will he?"

"Probably not," Alex said as he squeezed her shoulder. "He's responding very well."

Alex would miss her, but he couldn't ask her to stay for that reason.

"Enjoy your dinner, then," Maryann said as if everything was settled.

Alex stopped himself before he answered. He'd grown accustomed to having her by his side and almost said as much. She was right, though. There was no real reason for her to stay with him.

So he nodded. "I don't think Timmy will be ready to go back until late in the day on

Thursday. Max said he'll make a trip whenever the hospital releases the boy."

"Well, that's good then," Maryann said. He looked over and saw she had opened her Bible.

"You'll need better light," he said as he walked over and unclipped the lamp from the top of Timmy's bed. He brought it closer to her. He hooked the lamp on the metal chain hanging from the window blinds. The cord still stretched to the plug-in, so he clicked it on. "There, that'll do."

It wouldn't pass the hospital safety check, but the cord was well out of the way of anyone walking around Timmy's bed.

"Thank you," Maryann said, looking up.

She was perfectly polite to him and his heart sank. Something was wrong. Alex thought they had gotten past his earlier awkwardness, but apparently not.

"If you'd rather go someplace other than the beach, that's okay," Alex said softly. "I'll take you any place you want."

He should have known. People always said they were giving someone else a new start, but it rarely happened in his experience. It had become a politically correct pretense in these past few years that all should be forgiven. But in reality, it was never that simple. Forgiveness needed to be earned; no one knew that better than him.

"You don't need to take me anywhere," Maryann said.

"But I want to."

Maryann turned her face slightly and the light from the lamp showed her eyes clearly. She was serious. "We'll talk about it later."

"I'm not suggesting we take off for the beach when Timmy's in the shape he's in, but we don't have much time," Alex said.

"I know," Maryann said as she looked back down at the Bible she still held. "But for now—enjoy your dinner."

Alex figured they would sound like strangers to anyone close enough to listen. The thought made him lose his appetite. He wondered if this is the way it would be for the next few weeks, until he left. If that was so, maybe he should stop at the pharmacy and get some antacids, because the prospect made him feel sour inside.

"I'll see you later," Alex said as he walked toward the door.

Chapter Nine

By the time Maryann stepped out of Max's floatplane and onto his dock the next morning, the sky had cleared. Everyone at the Juneau airport had commented that it was such a sunny day, saying they didn't get that many nice ones this far into the month of September. Maryann wouldn't have cared if they'd announced a hailstorm was under way; she'd smiled politely and agreed with whatever anyone said about the weather.

Then she'd hitched the strap of her purse higher on her shoulder and continued walking to the plane. She'd wanted to get home. That was the place she was at peace—Treasure Creek.

The flight had taken fifty-nine minutes.

She was so happy to be back in the small town, she almost skipped off the dock and kissed the earth at her feet. The only problem was that it was Max's dirt, and he already thought she was more thrilled with him than she was. Not that he wasn't a perfectly fine man and a conscientious pilot. It's just that he smiled too much. She took a moment to ponder how that could be. Surely she wasn't against smiles. But every time he broke forth with one, it seemed he expected her to smile right back at him. By the time they landed, her jaw was tired.

"You're welcome to fly to Juneau with me anytime you want," Max said as he stood on his dock with his legs braced against any possible movement, looking as if he was the captain of the sea. "No charge. I'll let you ride in the copilot seat. I don't usually have a passenger sit there anyway, so it's no loss to me."

"Thank you. That's most kind." She stopped. Then she smiled at him because that seemed the only polite thing to do after such a magnificent offer. It was worth hundreds of dollars, and she wished she could get more enthusiastic about it.

She started to turn to leave, but Max wasn't done yet.

"Some weekend we could fly down, just the two of us, and catch a movie in that new theater on Front Street." He continued with such confidence, she knew he didn't expect to be refused. "Maybe have some dinner at this Thai place one of the other pilots told me about—you know, have a good time."

Unfortunately, she did know.

"I'm afraid I'll be busy most weekends until the doctor leaves." She didn't bother to attempt a smile. "I'll be going through patient files, making sure everything is ready for the next doctor."

Max frowned. "Alex shouldn't make you work like that. Everyone needs some time off."

"Yes, well… "Maryann murmured as she turned. This time she kept walking as she spoke. "Maybe it'll be better next spring."

And maybe there would be a heat wave at Christmas, she thought. *And diamonds in everyone's stockings. And*—she stopped herself. In all fairness, she needed to ease up on Max. He wasn't the one who had upset her, anyway.

It was the other arrogant man of the day. *Him.*

This morning she had woken, sitting upright in that hospital chair, with a red silk rose and the keys to the Jeep in her lap. The nurse, who had been making up the bed in the room, said Alex had gone with Doctor Stuart and Timmy, to run some more tests on the boy. He'd left word Maryann was to use his Jeep to get back to town from the dock where Max would land his floatplane.

Without thinking, she had brushed the silk rose across her cheek, just to feel its softness. That's when she was hit by the wave of anger. Why would Alex give her a rose, when he was leaving? He probably already had his boxes packed and his reservations made. In two weeks, he'd start forwarding his mail. It was too late for silk flowers. Sure he'd invited her to dinner, but the man was leaving. He should have done something weeks ago if he had any feelings for her. Which he obviously didn't.

The very thought made her turn half of that anger on herself. She was the one who had dived into this confused mess of emotions all by herself. If she wanted to have a peaceful, smooth relationship with someone, she needed to keep her emotions in check.

Just two days ago, she had everything under control. He was The Ice Man and she was the nurse. The only reason she had cared if Alex left Treasure Creek was because of the children.

All of those thoughts raced to a stop when Max—the handsome, generous pilot—appeared in the doorway of the hospital room. He had flown Mrs. Fields back to be with her son. He informed Maryann that he was in a hurry to make the return flight, and if she wanted a ride, she'd have to hurry. He was impatient, confident—a man all too sure of himself. Just like someone else she knew.

So she had picked up the Jeep keys, tossed the rose into the trash and said she was ready to go. She told Mrs. Fields to explain to Timmy that she was flying back to Treasure Creek. Within fifteen minutes, she and Max were in a cab going to the airport. She'd been annoyed with Max the whole flight. It was unfair, and she didn't think he'd noticed, but it was the truth.

And now she was on the outskirts of her small town, walking toward Alex's Jeep. The keys opened the driver's door and she was inside in seconds. She drove slowly—the last thing she wanted was to hit something while driving a borrowed vehicle—but she still made it past the welcome-to-town sign in less than ten minutes.

She pulled into the large space behind Lindy's Boarding House. Her seldom-used car was where she had left it, over by the trees. The area in the back of the boarding house was graveled to keep down the mud, and there were no clear parking spaces. At this time of day there were only a few other vehicles around, so no one paid much attention to who parked where.

As she walked toward the house, she faced the one unit with an entrance off the back. It was a ground-level apartment that had been the maids' quarters a hundred years ago. Maryann noticed there were now curtains in the windows. She wondered if Lindy had finally been persuaded to rent the double room plus bath to one of the tenants who had been begging for it. She had been keeping it vacant in the hope that she would find someone willing to rent it in exchange for giving her help with the cooking, and, as Lindy delicately referred to it, the guest management part of her job. That was the rent collection, noise control and complaint departments.

Maryann told herself she'd go up to her room to change clothes and then she'd ask Lindy if there were any leftovers she could have for a late breakfast. Within a half hour, she'd be down to the clinic, rescheduling tomorrow's appointments. She'd leave the ones for Friday in place, as Alex would probably be back in time for them.

She walked around the side of the building

and climbed the steps to the wide porch. The wicker rocking chairs were still there. In a few weeks, they would be put in storage for the winter. She opened the main door to the boarding house and, as always, triggered the ringing of the tiny bell that hung over the door. Something smelled good, and bursts of laughter were coming from the rooms in back.

Maryann closed the door and Lindy herself appeared in the hallway, coming out of the kitchen.

"You're home," Lindy said with a great deal of warmth as she walked toward her. "And I hear Timmy Fields is doing much better."

Lindy had her blond hair pulled back into a ponytail, a blue-checked full apron tied over her jeans and a white T-shirt. She had flour on her hands and a streak of it on her cheek. She looked cream puff sweet, but she made no secret of the fact that she'd come from a rough background. She never knew her father, and her mother had spent most of Lindy's childhood in jail for one thing or another.

"I'd hug you, but I'm all full of dough," Lindy said, her eyes shining.

"I see that, and, yes, Timmy is doing much, much better," Maryann said as she leaned in and gave Lindy a loose hug anyway. "I hope all that flour means you're making biscuits. I'm starving."

Lindy laughed. "I owe you more than biscuits. Name it and I'll make it for dinner—if I have the ingredients. Chicken cordon bleu, ostrich burgers, crab chowder. I forget…what are your favorites?"

With that, Lindy started back to the kitchen.

"Is this about Timmy?" Maryann asked, trying to figure out why her landlady was making her a special dinner. Granted, Maryann had gone with the boy to the hospital, but she could hardly claim a hero's reward. The doctors and nurses in Juneau, with Alex's help, had pulled the boy through.

Lindy stopped in midstep and turned around. "I guess you don't know? Oh, I assumed he'd told you."

Maryann looked at her blankly.

"You got me a new tenant," Lindy explained, her face glowing. "He said you spoke highly of my place. He called when he was on the plane coming into town, and asked if he could rent something for a few weeks."

Maryann's heart sank. Surely she hadn't mentioned anything to Max. She knew he was looking for an apartment, but she hadn't thought he'd be content with a room.

"I'm renting him the maids' quarters," Lindy continued, looking pleased with herself. "I've decided no one's going to peel potatoes and dust for me anyway. At least, not right now. And he needed the door back there."

The private entrance in the rear of the house had been built extra wide for the laundry that used to pass through, so it could be hung on the clothesline just feet from the door.

"I'm sure he'll be very happy here," Maryann said. It was now official; Max was the most charming man in the whole state of Alaska. No one else could have talked Lindy out of her dream of a maid.

"I hope he is happy," Lindy said, her voice low so it didn't carry far. "I am, too. He's in the kitchen right now, folding napkins for dinner. He knows a million things about cooking. I felt bad letting him help out like this, but he said he wanted to put all those cooking shows he's watched on television to good use. He's going to show me how to braise things. Just as soon as we finish making these orange cranberry rolls for tomorrow."

"Max?" Maryann asked. She couldn't picture the pilot working in Lindy's kitchen. And how would he have gotten here that fast from his plane, anyway. Then she realized. "It's not Max, is it?"

"No. He said you know him though. Rocco Frank is his name." Lindy's face lit up with pride. "Isn't that the most handsome-sounding name ever?"

Maryann was stunned. She stood and stared at Lindy.

"Somebody must be playing a practical joke," she finally said. "Rocco wouldn't just show up here. How could he get here without us knowing? Alex said he never traveled. And that's not his real name anyway."

All of the light drained from Lindy's face. "Not his real name? He's not hiding from the law, is he? I never thought to ask that. When he said he knew you, I just assumed—I should have known better. I'm a magnet for trouble."

"No, no. It's nothing like that," Maryann assured her as she reached out to put a hand on the other woman's shoulder. "He's a model citizen as far as I know. He's just—well, he's in a wheelchair and—"

"There's nothing wrong with being in a wheelchair—nothing," Lindy said, her color coming back. "I have a stepsister in a wheelchair. Besides, President Roosevelt was in a wheelchair. And what's his name—the man who's a genius?"

"Stephen Hawking."

"Yeah, that's him."

"Of course there's nothing wrong with people being in wheelchairs. Unless they let it stop them from doing things. And Alex said his brother didn't even go to the grocery store." Maryann wanted to lie down in a dark room and put a cold washcloth on her forehead. "Can I see the man?"

Lindy looked at her, measuring her.

"If you're sure you won't make him feel uncomfortable," Lindy finally said. "I've never had anyone offer to help in the kitchen before. Well, at least not with something like folding napkins. He's making swans."

"I'll be warm and welcoming to him," Maryann said, with a smile. "No matter who he is."

Lindy nodded. "Good. And since you're hungry, I can make you a meatloaf sandwich while we're back there."

"I missed meatloaf night?" Maryann asked as she followed Lindy through the wide hallway and back to the kitchen. "Why do I always miss my favorite?"

"So that's it. Your favorite," Lindy said as she stopped in the doorway to the kitchen.

Maryann looked over the other woman's shoulder. There was indeed a man in a wheelchair leaning over a short table someone had set up in the corner. He had a couple of dozen cloth napkins stacked on the table, and he was folding them into all kinds of shapes. He had some white ones that looked like chef hats.

The man turned to look at them.

Maryann didn't need more than a glance to know he was Alex's older brother. The two of them shared the same shape to their nose and jawline. Of course, a few old scars marred the skin on Rocco's face, and it was obvious he hadn't spent much time in the sun in the past years. His hair had some gray in it, but it had the same fullness that Alex's had. And there was an almost identical tilt to the head when they were listening for something.

"Rocco?" Maryann finally asked. She swallowed. How had he managed to end up in Lindy's kitchen?

He looked at her and squinted. "Nurse Jenner? You sound like Nurse Jenner."

"I need to sit down." Maryann stared at him for another minute. Then she walked over and pulled a chair out to sit down at the table with him.

"How did you get here?" she finally asked. "I mean, Alex has told me you never left the house." She stopped to swallow. "This is a pretty major trip."

"It's amazing what a few calls can get you."

"I see you figured it all out," Maryann said, starting to be proud of him.

Rocco nodded. "Direct flight. You leave Los Angeles, take a short nap, and before you know it, you're in Alaska. At least Anchorage. That's what gave me the idea of coming up here. I could hardly get lost when, from start to finish, I'd be on the same plane."

Maryann looked around. She'd forgotten he was a young teen when he'd been hit by the car. "And you managed to get here from Anchorage."

"It was simple." He seemed pleased. "I flew down to Juneau and arranged for a private plane to pick me up. The pilot, Max, delivered me right to Lindy's place."

Bless Max's heart for thinking of Lindy's empty maids' quarters, a place that could easily accommodate Rocco's wheelchair. But still…"I heard you had an attendant. Didn't he come with you?"

Rocco shook his head. "I sent him on vacation for a few days. He' been teaching me how to do things for myself, but it's not a real test if he's there to rescue me."

"I suppose," Maryann said.

Rocco bent his head down and folded a

napkin. This one appeared to be in the shape of a star. Maryann started to stand.

Then he looked at her again. "My brother's going to be mad, isn't he?"

"You didn't tell him you were coming, did you?" she asked, even though she knew the answer.

Rocco shook his head. "He kind of—what do you think he'll say?"

"Well, I don't know. I expect he'll be surprised. Very surprised."

"It wasn't as hard as I always thought it would be." Rocco gave a small, satisfied smile. "The people on the airplane were really nice."

"I'm glad—and I'm sure your brother will be grateful, too, when you tell him."

Rocco looked back down at the napkins he was folding, and it made Maryann uneasy. "You have left a message for your brother that you're in town, haven't you? I know he picks up messages from his home phone when he's away."

Rocco shook his head without looking up. "I thought I should rest up first."

"Oh," Maryann said.

"Don't worry," Rocco continued. "I'll tell him—soon." He thought for a moment. "Maybe Friday."

"Friday!" Maryann protested. "Today's Wednesday. You can't possibly plan to hide out all day tomorrow and wait to see him Friday."

Rocco shrugged. "I just want to see if I can be on my own for a couple of days. Lindy will let me help in the kitchen in exchange for meals, and I can roll my wheelchair out my door and see the mountains. Lindy says there's a moose that's been coming to town around dusk each night. What I wouldn't give to see a moose."

"Yes, but—" Maryann started, and then remembered the first time she'd seen a live moose.

"If Alex knows I'm here," Rocco interrupted, "He'll make me move into his place and try to do everything for me. It's time for me to take care of myself for a change. Please don't tell him I'm here. Not yet."

Maryann shook her head. She knew just how he felt. "I won't lie to him, but I won't call him in Juneau and tell him either. He's bound to find out when he gets back to town, though.

Rocco nodded with a grin. "That's why I haven't been using my last name. You're the only one who knows Alex is my brother."

"Wonderful," Maryann muttered. She really

did need to lie down for a few minutes before she went to the clinic.

"I'll be grateful to you forever," Rocco said.

She sighed. "I don't think he'll be back here before Thursday, late afternoon."

Since it was Wednesday morning and Alex couldn't do anything until Friday anyway, that gave Rocco two days.

"I sure hope that moose comes around tonight." Rocco said. "And maybe a bear would come to town, too. I've never seen a bear either."

"Bears don't usually—" she started, and then stopped. "If I see one, I'll come down and knock on your door."

A day really wasn't too much to ask of life, she thought, as she started to push her chair out so she could stand. Alex would just have to cope with it. She had no doubt he'd find out eventually that she had known and not called him.

"Not so fast," Lindy said, as she walked over to the table. "I just made you the best meatloaf sandwich of your life. I used my imported mustard and some of that home-canned relish I got at the farmer's market at Harry's last summer."

"It looks wonderful," Maryann said as she

sat back down and looked at the thick sandwich. She just wished it didn't have the feel of being her last meal. Alex might be more angry with her than with his brother. In fact, he might think she encouraged his brother to come up here, with all of her talk about how the mountains were so beautiful and the air so fresh.

For someone seeking a peaceful life, she was sure managing to stir up trouble. She cut the sandwich in half and gestured for Rocco to have some. When he took it, she knew she'd at least made a friend today.

Chapter Ten

Alex was in the copilot seat of Max's float-plane, headed down to Treasure Creek from Juneau. It was late afternoon on Wednesday and the sun was beginning to set. Alex hadn't felt much like talking since they left the hospital.

"I bet you'll be glad to be home," Max said as he began to turn his plane so he could approach his dock for landing. "I know I will be."

Alex grunted. He needed clean clothes and a shave. Timmy and his mother were wrapped in blankets in the backseat and sound asleep—which reminded him that he needed a nap, too. The last two days had been a roller coaster of despair and jubilation. But it was worth it. Timmy was going to be all right.

"I hope you don't mind that I called ahead

to let Amy know we're bringing Timmy home today instead of tomorrow," Max said as he shifted something on his control panel. "She'd called earlier and left a message. I have a feeling she wants to organize something."

"Of course I don't mind," Alex said a little surprised it was even a question. Maybe he'd been a little too silent on this trip. "The boy deserves a hero's welcome after what he's been through. He won't be able to stay for the celebration, though. He needs to be home in bed."

The boy had not only survived pneumonia, he'd pulled through with his faith intact, Alex marveled. The boy really thought God was there for him.

It was the Twenty-third Psalm that had made that clear. Earlier today, after they did the last of the tests, Timmy had asked Alex for that Bible again.

Alex knew where the book was, because this morning Maryann had left it on the shelf by Timmy's bed. Unlike the rose she'd left in the trash, which had obviously been discarded, he was sure the Bible had been merely forgotten. By the time he opened it to where the blue candy wrapper had been placed earlier, he realized Timmy didn't even need the written words. The boy already had his eyes closed tight and was repeating the psalm from memory.

"The Lord is my shepherd," Timmy mumbled. Then he opened his eyes and looked directly into Alex's eyes. "It's better if two people say it together." Then he held out his hand and took Alex's in his own.

Alex was surprised he remembered the words, but together they managed to haltingly make their way through the psalm. It was just as well he wasn't reading it, Alex told himself halfway through, since he wouldn't be able to see the words anyway due to the tears in his eyes anyway. Saying these words with Timmy affected him. At first he thought it was because he was remembering how he'd shared the boy's feelings at one time and was feeling nostalgic.

But, by the middle of the psalm, Alex realized his big problem wasn't even with God. It was with himself. The day Rocco had saved his life was the day Alex no longer felt like he deserved to be in contact with God. He felt like he should be banished, not welcomed. Maybe he would have gotten over that feeling, but everything in his family also changed that day.

They stopped going to church. They no longer prayed before meals. To Alex, it was as though he had led his whole family out into the wilderness. He believed his family was sharing his apartness from God, giving rise to the suspicion that maybe they knew something he didn't about his lack of closeness to God after all that had happened. Not that he had blamed God for any of it; it was just the way things were.

They had finished the psalm before Alex even realized it.

"Don't cry," Timmy whispered. "Everything's going to be okay."

Alex opened his eyes and nodded, even though he didn't believe Timmy's words. Not anymore. Too many years separated the man he was today from the faith he had as a boy. Besides, a man was called to be more accountable than a child, even if it would be nice to feel there were no hard feelings between him and God. Maybe he should try to resolve things. There should be something he could do that would make God's heart soften toward him.

Amy said that the church needed a new organ. Maybe once he earned enough to build that clinic, he'd send a check to the Treasure Creek church so they could get a new organ. That should get God's attention and make Alex feel like he could talk to Him again.

* * *

Max dropped the plane down and landed next to that special dock of his.

"If you give me a minute, I can get my ramp elevated so we can carry the boy down. I had a man in a wheelchair use it yesterday. The ramp worked like a charm," Max said as he turned off all the knobs on his panel. "We had the guy out of here and down to the dock in minutes."

"Good for him," Alex said, thinking of his brother. Now why couldn't Rocco try something like that? He needn't make such a big trip, of course, but he could at least get out of the house. Rocco had his attendant; the man was supposed to help him learn to get around better. Rocco should at least be wheeling himself out to the curb.

Alex had checked his messages a couple of times yesterday. He had expected Rocco to leave a few words acknowledging it was his birthday. But if Rocco called he didn't leave a message.

Mr. Fields was there with the car, to give everyone a ride into Treasure Creek. Alex squeezed into the backseat with Timmy on his lap.

"You'll want to give this back to Maryann," Mrs. Fields said as she turned from the front seat and held out the white Bible to him. "I know she sets great store by it."

"That she does," Alex agreed as he took it back. The sky had darkened, but Alex could still see the edges of that old map in the middle of the Bible.

He noticed Timmy eyeing the Bible, too.

"I figure maybe you can come to the clinic tomorrow for a checkup," Alex said to the boy. "That'll give us a chance to discuss things."

Timmy nodded, his eyes wide.

"I didn't mean any harm," he whispered, with a glance at his parents sitting in the front seat.

"I know. We'll talk about it tomorrow," Alex said.

When Mr. Fields turned onto the main thoroughfare of Treasure Creek, Alex looked down the street. There was a light on at the clinic. The stress of the day eased out of him. Maryann must be there still.

"You can let me off at the clinic," Alex said to Mr. Fields.

"I was hoping you'd want to stop by Lizbet's with us," the other man answered. "We've been invited over to celebrate Timmy's homecoming. We won't stay, of course. But Timmy can hear the cheers through the car window."

"I'll be over later," Alex said.

The man nodded. "I want you to know I'm much obliged for what you did for us. My wife told me you talked the hospital into giving us credit. I plan to call them tomorrow and make arrangements. The missus didn't have time to stop in and ask them about payments."

Alex froze. "I didn't really—well, about the payments—the hospital doesn't really…"

Mr. Fields stopped his car in front of the clinic. "We're here now."

"When you bring Timmy in tomorrow for his appointment," Alex said to Mr. Fields, "we'll talk about everything then. It's just—well, don't worry. The finances will be all right."

The other man nodded and Alex opened the car door. Then he said a quick goodbye to everyone and, Bible in hand, stepped out of the car and walked toward the clinic. He was glad he had the book with him, since he knew Maryann would be happy to have that returned to her, even if she might have problems with him showing up sooner than she expected. He wished he could convince himself there was some benign reason for that rose to have been in the waste basket in Timmy's room. It sure didn't build a man's confidence.

Alex opened the door and took a moment to enjoy the astonishment on his nurse's face when she saw he was there. She was sitting at the receptionist desk, the lamp behind her putting out a yellow light that gave her brown hair a shine. She didn't have her usual white uniform on. In fact, she was wearing a rose-colored sweater and some silver earrings. All in all, she looked very nice—too nice for work.

"You're back?" Maryann finally seemed to find her voice.

"Timmy was okay to come home earlier than we thought," Alex said, as he walked over to her desk and set the Bible down. "Brought this back to you. The map's still there. Timmy's coming in tomorrow and we'll have our talk. Amy will want to be here, too."

Maryann nodded and swallowed. "I'm sure the boy didn't mean any harm."

Alex frowned. Unless he was mistaken, Maryann was nervous around him. There was no reason she would be, unless...

"You're worried I'll get the boy in trouble with his father, aren't you?" he asked. "I can assure you I won't."

Maryann shook her head. "I can't imagine his parents will be too upset with him after what he's been through. He's only eight years old."

Something still wasn't right, Alex told himself. He knew she cared about the boy. He wondered who else she cared about.

"Max called, didn't he?" Alex finally asked. "And said…what?"

Maryann shook her head.

There could only be one other thing, Alex thought. "Don't tell me you set me up with one of the fancy women?"

"No, it's not that," she said.

He was completely out of theories, Alex admitted to himself. "Well, whatever it is, it can't be that bad. Just tell me. Come over to the diner with me and we can talk while we have some pizza."

Maryann smiled and finally looked him in the eyes. "I'll come for pizza, but I still can't tell you anything. I promised I wouldn't. Not until tomorrow—if you don't know by tomorrow evening, I can probably say something."

"Probably?" He lifted an eyebrow.

"I'd have to ask the other person first."

Alex felt a sudden stab of jealousy. "It's not Max, is it?"

Maryann shook her head emphatically. "And no more guessing. Not that you'd guess right anyway, but…"

As long as she wasn't going to announce that she was running off to be Max's full-time copilot, he figured he could wait to know what she was talking about. Women sometimes liked to have their secrets, and he consoled himself with that certainty.

"Nice hair," he said as she stood up and reached behind the desk for her coat. "You've done something different, haven't you? Added those—what do you call them—'lights'?"

"Highlights?" Maryann said as she turned around, her coat in hand. "No, I don't have highlights."

Alex stepped over to help her with her coat. As he did so, he said, "Well, highlights would be wasted on you. Your hair is beautiful just the way it is."

"Thank you," Maryann said as she slipped her arms into her coat. Then she looked up at him with mischief on her face. "I'm still not going to tell you what you want to know, though. Not until the end of work tomorrow. And then only if I get permission."

Her face was so alive that he almost kissed her. Then he remembered the last time they'd almost kissed and how conversation had stopped for the rest of the evening. And tonight he wanted to talk to her and hear her laugh.

He did put his arm around her shoulders as they walked through the door though.

"It's dark out here," Alex said, as she looked up at him. "Wouldn't want you to trip."

She seemed to accept that explanation, because she didn't pull away. They walked down the stairs in harmony.

"I wonder if that old moose will show up tonight?" Alex said as they started to walk down the street.

He felt Maryann's shoulders tense beneath his arm. He supposed the reason he had thought of that animal was because they saw it on their previous walk together. He didn't want her to feel uncomfortable about that, though.

"It's not very likely," Alex said. "They don't come out as much as they used to."

"He could be there," Maryann declared. "I hope he is."

Alex was now thoroughly confused. Not that he minded the feeling, since he was walking down the street with Maryann on his arm.

"The stars should be out tonight, too," he ventured to add. "A little later, that is."

Maryann worried as they walked down the street. What if Rocco was out taking a tour of the town? In the little bit of time she'd spent with him earlier, she had decided he had become fearless. Of course, if she only had one day to look around paradise, she supposed she would be curious to see what it was all like, too.

They made it all the way to the General Store before Alex said anything. "I suppose you like things that are alive instead of, well, not?" he asked with such a studied casualness that she knew it was anything but that.

"What?" She stopped to look up at him in confusion. "I'm a nurse. Of course I like things to be alive. What kind of a question is that? Are you saying I don't take my job seriously?"

Enough light streamed through the large glass pane window of the store that she could see Alex's face. He had dark stubble on his face from not shaving for a couple of days. And his hair was tousled, as though he hadn't been combing it that much. He had the faint air of someone who was haunted by something. He looked more like a biker than a doctor. And the whole combination was way too appealing for her.

"I *do*—take my job seriously," she repeated, when she found her voice again—even though, from the look on his face, she had already figured out that that wasn't what he was talking about at all.

"It's the rose," he finally muttered, just as she was afraid he would.

"I thought maybe you only liked fresh ones," he added. "If they had any real flowers in the gift shop, I would have gotten you one of those instead."

Maryann's mouth went dry. She hadn't meant for him to see the rose. She thought the orderly who was making the bed would empty the trash as well.

"I—ah—I," she stammered, "I do like the fresh ones better. That's true."

She took a breath to tell him the real reason she hadn't liked the silk flower, but when she opened her mouth nothing came out. He was looking at her so intently. His eyes darkened until they looked warm and caring. She forgot for a moment what she was supposed to say.

"I—ah—I…" She took another run at it, but only produced a breathless squeak. Finally she settled for, "I'm sorry. Truly sorry."

He smiled and his whole face turned boyish. "Just as long as it's only the rose you don't like."

And then he turned to begin walking again. This time he cuddled her more closely under his arm, and she didn't say anything. Alex's brother wasn't the only one who was exploring new territory tonight, she told herself. She knew full well that the fantasy she was living while walking down this street would expire in a couple of weeks. She figured her emotions would be in upheaval until Alex left, and then she'd know bleakness for days or weeks. It would be worth it though, she knew.

Chapter Eleven

The light on the porch outside of Lizbet's Diner had burned out, so the steps were hidden by the growing shadows of nearby buildings. The night was getting darker and colder. Even with her jacket on, Maryann was grateful for Alex's arm around her shoulder as they made their way to the top of the wide porch. Besides, she liked being this close to him.

"So, when do you leave again?" she asked, just to remind herself of reality.

He didn't answer for a bit, then he said, "The twenty-seventh. That's a Saturday. I take the red eye flight out of Anchorage, down to Los Angeles."

She nodded. Sixteen more days. The answer helped numb her feelings. She needed some perspective; he was still leaving. Maybe he would say something about keeping in touch or coming back to visit. But maybe he'd say nothing. People tended to leave acquaintances more easily than they used to in earlier days. Her parents had taught her that. "Out with the old and in with the new"—that was their motto.

"I keep meaning to stop by Harry's store and post a sign on his bulletin board to sell my Jeep," Alex added quietly. "I bought it used when I first got here, and I don't know what I would do with it if I drove it down to Los Angeles. The roads are so different down there. Faster, more congested. And the freeways…"

Maryann nodded. Everything would be new for him when he moved. "Someone's sure to buy your Jeep when you're gone. And they'll treasure it like it deserves."

She shouldn't have added the last. It revealed too much about her heart, but he didn't seem to notice. He was leaving her behind, too, though. That much was growing clear.

The light shifted inside the diner, like maybe someone had turned on a couple more bulbs, and the light streaming out was mellow and golden. Maryann felt like she was in one of those old forties movies, where everyone wore hats and there was always some man saying goodbye to the woman he loved, because he had to make good on some promise, instead of standing by her side.

Maryann took a deep breath. She had never understood why those women wept over their men. If the men didn't want to stay, who needed them? A true man found a way to take his woman with him. Or he stayed behind. She could understand wartime, but for Alex it was a clinic.

She stopped herself. She was not going to be sad or angry tonight. She looked up at Alex and smiled. Rocco had already taught her something at the kitchen table this morning. She was going to live today to the full.

Just then Linda, one of the uniformed waitresses, opened the door and came outside with a light bulb in her hand and a slight frown on her face.

"Oh, it is dark out here," she said, fretting as she stood beneath the light fixture. "Nobody's paying me for this. Someone said we needed a new light, and I just got elected to change it." The waitress turned to look at Maryann and Alex. "Do I look like an electrician to either of you?"

"No," Alex said and held out his hand for the bulb.

"I'm no electrician either," he said when

Linda opened her mouth to protest. "But I am taller, and I can reach the fixture without you needing to get a ladder."

"Thank you, then," the woman said as she gave him the bulb. "You're all right, you know? For a doctor, that is. You're not stuck-up or anything."

"Thank you." Alex screwed in the new bulb.

Light flooded the porch. Maryann blinked.

Then Alex opened the door for them and they walked inside. The diner was overflowing with people, half of them standing and half of them seated at tables. People were laughing and having a good time.

Linda nodded at the two of them and went back to work.

Someone gave a shrill whistle and Maryann looked over to see Max, sitting at a small round table, and waving toward them.

"Guess we should go over," Alex said.

The smell of pizza and grilled hamburgers filled the air as Maryann and Alex side-stepped their way to the table where Max was. It wasn't easy to move through the crowd, since almost everyone wanted to slap Alex on the back and tell him he'd done a good job for their little Timmy. He smiled and nodded to them all.

"Hey, there," Max said when they got close enough to hear. "Sorry there aren't many empty seats."

At that moment Max and Alex both looked at the one empty chair.

Max started to stand, then sat back down, a grin covering his face. "Maryann can sit on my knee. She doesn't weigh but a bit."

"She can take the chair. I'll stand," Alex retorted as he guided Maryann to the empty chair.

Max gave a low chuckle. Alex knew, without looking at the man's face, that he'd been hoping Maryann would perch herself on his leg while she ate. But that would never happen.

Alex nodded in satisfaction to no one in particular. He was glad Maryann was safely sitting in her own place. He leaned down and put a hand on the back of her neck.

"What would you like me to order for you?" he whispered in her ear. He could smell her floral shampoo and feel wisps of hair along her neckline where his thumb rested. He'd never noticed before how delicate her earlobes were. "Maybe some hot green tea?"

She turned her face to look up at him, and

suddenly it felt as if the fifty or sixty people in the room had disappeared and there were only the two of them. She met his eyes in surprise. "How'd you know that's what I'd like?"

"You drink a cup every day at your desk."

"I didn't know you paid any attention," she said.

Alex hadn't known he'd noticed as much as he had about Maryann, either. His previous nurse had worked with him for much longer, and he couldn't remember what *she* liked to drink at her desk. But he could fill a notebook with things about Maryann. The way she liked to stop in front of the window and tilt her head up at the mountains. The way she lifted her eyebrows when she disagreed with him. And the way her lips curled just so when he said something that amused her.

"I've noticed more than I realized," he finally said, bending close enough to her ear so only she would hear him.

A woman cleared her throat and Alex looked up to see the waitress, Linda, standing beside him with her order pad in her hand. He looked across the table and saw Max with a stunned look on his face.

"Decided to come back to earth and join us?" Max asked, but here was no rancor in his voice.

"It's been a long day," Alex said as he straightened to his full height.

"You know what you want?" Linda asked. "I've got a full house here."

Alex nodded and ordered tea for Maryann and sodas for him and Max. Then he looked around. The place was filled with plates of nachos dripping with processed cheese, and hamburgers with double sides of mayonnaise. People were eating as if they were bears ready to hibernate for the winter.

"What do you put on your vegetable pizza?" he asked.

"Onions, red peppers, mushrooms and olives."

"Any tomatoes?"

"We haven't gotten our fresh delivery yet," Linda said. "It comes on the early-morning plane."

Alex nodded. "We'll take your biggest size, and bring a salad with it."

"There's nothing but lettuce. But we do have some coleslaw."

"That'll do," Alex said.

Just then a loud bell rang out. Everyone knew that meant someone wanted to say something. Sure enough, Amy climbed up on a chair so the whole diner could see her, then she started to talk.

Alex wasn't really listening. He was paying more attention to Maryann's hair. Several strands of her hair curled around her ear—strands that had escaped the discipline of her brush.

Then Alex heard his name and his attention was caught by Amy's speech.

"…our very own Dr. Havens got Timmy to the hospital in time to save his life." There was a smattering of applause at this, and Alex waved at people to stop. Instead, they got louder. Finally someone rang the bell again.

Amy continued. "As you know, hospitals are not cheap, and the Fields family will have a big bill soon." There was a wave of murmurs at this. It gave Alex a bad feeling, since he was the only one there who knew there was nothing due on Timmy's bill.

The bell rang again, and Amy continued. "Everyone's invited to the fellowship hall of the Treasure Creek Christian Church this Saturday for a pancake and caribou sausage breakfast. The proceeds will go to The Timmy Fields Fund, to help pay off that bill. Mr. Fields will let us know on Saturday just how much we need to collect, so bring your wallets and don't be shy about opening them up for our own Timmy Fields." People cheered.

Alex didn't feel any better than Timmy

probably did about now. It hadn't occurred to him that the town would start raising money for the bill he'd already paid. He hadn't planned to tell anyone what he had done. He hadn't really thought about what the Fields family would think. If anything, he figured they'd think the hospital had forgotten them somehow. And since they had a hard enough time paying the bills that came to their door, he thought they'd just forget the one that didn't.

Alex had had no idea all the people in town would be involved. They knew about the clinic he was building for his brother in Los Angeles, and he didn't want them to worry that he wouldn't be able to do it now. It would be different if they could earn enough money at their breakfast to cover the bill, but they'd do well to raise a few hundred dollars. And if they went to the hospital with the money in hand to make a payment, they would know the bill was paid.

The cheering died down.

"Your order's here," the waitress said as she slapped a wire holder on the table with one hand and then lowered the big tray of pizza with the other. "I'll be back with your drinks."

"Smells good," Max said from where he'd

moved his chair. The other man hadn't pushed his chair as close to Maryann as he could, and Alex felt as if they'd turned some corner. He couldn't thank Max right now, though.

So instead Alex took a deep whiff of the pizza smell. It had been a long time since he'd had a slice of pizza. Then he looked around at the children watching him. Some of them were from Treasure Creek and some from the Tlingit village. He glanced down at Maryann and saw she was watching him being scrutinized by the children, too. She looked up with a smile for him and whispered. "Little eyes. They want to see what the doctor eats."

Alex nodded. Then he held out a hand to Max and one to Maryann.

"Let's pray," he said. Somewhere in the time he'd spent with Timmy, he'd grown convinced that the children in his medical care needed spiritual health as well. He planned to talk to Reverend Michaels about that when he got a chance. In the meantime, he needed some help. "Maryann, will you lead us in prayer?"

She was surprised. He could see that plainly. But she looked around at the gawking children and bowed her head anyway.

"Dear God," she began. "Thank You so much for making Timmy well again. We ask that You help us all to keep healthy. Help us to not cry when we get our shots and to brush our teeth after every meal. We thank You now for this food, especially the coleslaw the doctor is eating. Vegetables are important, and we thank You for them. Amen."

"Amen," Alex said with a smile. He leaned down and whispered to Maryann, "Thanks for the public-service announcements."

"Well, they should brush their teeth," Mary-ann said. Then she grinned at the children who had nudged closer, and added more loudly, "Just like I'm going to brush my teeth after I eat some of this pizza."

"Is it the vegetable?" a little voice asked. A Tlingit boy walked closer to the table, his brown eyes as big as the pizza he was starting at. "I've never had mushrooms before."

A couple of other Tlingit children edged closer, too. Alex noted that Max was getting a worried look on his face. The rules of village hospitality were very clear. Food was shared. Another child lined up at the table and the adults were outnumbered.

Alex motioned for Linda to come back.

"Yes?" she asked when she got there.

She frowned at the children. "Do your parents know you're over here begging pizza?"

They didn't answer, and she sighed and said, "Yeah, I suppose not."

"I'd like to order another pizza," Alex finally said. "Make it a big one just like this, only double the mushrooms."

"Gotcha," Linda said with a smile.

The pizza was gone all too soon. The children left, and half of the other diners had gone as well. Alex finally had a chair, so he could sit at the table with Max and Maryann. He did it, but he wasn't sure he wouldn't have preferred to stay crouched by her chair like her protector.

It didn't occur to Alex until they started to walk out that he'd meant to ask a question. He quickly excused himself and went in search of the waitress. She was back in the kitchen, filling a bowl of chili.

"That shipment you get in," he said to her. "Can you call tonight and add something to the order?"

"Sure we could," she said. "What do you need?"

"I was wondering if you could order me a dozen red roses to come in with your shipment. Real roses—nothing plastic or silk or chocolate. And make them the long stem kind. Deep red."

Linda set the bowl of chili down on the metal counter and a grin spread across her face. "A dozen long stem red roses? That sounds like you're trying to impress someone. I don't suppose you'd like to tell me who? I've got money riding on which of the fancy women you've got your eye on."

"I don't have my eye on any of them," he said, trying to be patient, because it would only make any gossip worse if he wasn't. "I just want some roses. What do I owe you?"

"I don't have a price," she said. "They'll be expensive, though. Maybe seventy or eighty dollars. Ninety even."

"Fine," he said. "Let me know when you want the money."

The waitress nodded. "Sure will. I'll call when the shipment comes in tomorrow. You can pay me when you pick them up."

Alex walked through the diner, looking for Maryann. She wasn't there, so he assumed Max had walked her home. But when he stepped out the door he saw her waiting on the porch.

She held up a white paper bag that held the leftover pizza. So that's why she'd waited. Still, a man took his chances when he could.

He grinned. "Want to take a walk?"

"I'm sure you're tired," she answered

hesitantly. "I just wanted to give you your pizza. And to say thank you. I liked that you bought the other pizza so the kids could have some, too."

Alex basked in her approval. "I'm not tired."

"Well then, I wouldn't say no to a short walk," she said with a smile as they both turned to walk off of the porch and down to the main road through town.

A few vehicles were parked alongside the asphalt road, and most of the businesses had dim lights showing through their windows, even though they were closed.

He took a moment before he moved in a little closer and put his arm around Maryann as they walked.

"Don't want you to get cold," he said, as though that was the reason. He hadn't noticed before how she was just the right height. She fit under his arm perfectly.

"You'll never see temperatures like these when you get back to Los Angeles," she said, sounding wistful.

"I'll miss it," he said, feeling pretty forlorn. He didn't want the evening to end like this, though, so he added, "Let's go see if we can find that moose anywhere around."

"Oh," Maryann stiffened. "I'm sure he's not

here. We really shouldn't even be out on the streets tonight."

"What?" Alex said, figuring he had missed a step, but he didn't know where. "I thought you liked that moose! It could be related to our Horace—you know, in the office?"

"I know Horace," she said, and then seemed at a loss. "I just realized that I'm a little tired after all. I really better get home."

"Well, I can at least walk you there," Alex said.

"Oh, no." She sounded truly alarmed. "I mean, there's no need. I'll see you tomorrow. Bright and early."

And with that she hurried away from him. There was nothing for him to do but to watch her dark shape as she walked down the street to the boarding house where she lived.

He stood in the middle of the almost empty street and shook his head. Maybe he did need to get some sleep. Nothing much made the kind of sense that it should. He watched until Maryann went into the door of the boarding house, and then he turned to walk back to his place. She was right, he would miss the cold bite of the air around here. He'd even miss Horace. But most of all he'd miss seeing Maryann's eyes light up when she saw an old moose walking around, or when—he stopped.

He hadn't realized until now that he wouldn't be here the first time Maryann saw an Alaskan snowstorm. Her whole face would radiate delight at that.

The price of doing his duty had finally climbed so high that he wasn't sure he could pay it.

Chapter Twelve

Maryann wore gloves the next morning, and it was still difficult to get the clinic's front door to open with her key. The lock was partially frozen. That sometimes happened when there was heavy dew the night before, and the temperatures fell. Last night had been cold, and according to Rocco, the moose had not shown up on the street in Treasure Creek.

Alex's brother had wheeled himself down the ramp of the boarding house many times during the early evening to look out at the street. Only Lindy's outspoken concern had kept him from rolling his wheelchair out onto the main road to go searching for the animal. She reminded him that moose might not be as interested in seeing Rocco as Rocco was in seeing the moose.

Maryann finally opened the door, and the

air inside was no warmer than outside. The cost of fuel oil was going up all the time, and at this time of year, no one kept their heater on overnight. When it got colder there would be concern for the pipes, so the heater would be left on, but just barely. That's why she kept her jacket on while she started her day.

The first thing she did was start the coffee brewing.

This morning, she looked through the list of appointments she'd rescheduled yesterday, to see if any of them would be ones she could rebook for their original time. She had ticked off four appointments when the phone rang.

"Hello," she answered. It was only ten minutes after eight. The clinic wasn't open for another twenty minutes. "Dr. Haven's office."

"Is he in?" a woman's voice asked. "It's Linda from the diner."

"Oh, hi Linda." Maryann relaxed when she knew who it was. "No, but he should be here before too long. Can I take a message?"

"Yeah, you can tell him that his flowers came in," Linda said. "They're ready for pickup."

Maryann tried to keep the pleasure from warming her. She knew he made that remark about replacing the silk rose with a real one, but she hadn't expected this. Then she told herself she couldn't assume anything was for her.

"What kind of flower?" she asked.

"Long stem red roses that would make you sit up and weep," Linda said, her voice dropping down in awe. "I keep wishing they were just a bouquet and not a dozen. There's no chance of stealing one on the sly. Twelve is twelve, and whoever gets these is going to count. At least, I would. Do you know which fancy woman they're for?"

Maryann stammered, "I—don't think—"

"I have twenty bucks on Delilah," the waitress said. "She might be a little overblown, but I think she's got a heart of gold."

"I'm sure she does, but—" Maryann started, but the waitress was already talking to someone on the side.

"Oops, gotta go," Linda said. "Someone didn't get their eggs sunny side up enough. Whatever enough means. Sunny side up or over easy—there's only two sides to an egg that's been fried."

"Well, I'll tell Dr. Havens about the flowers," Maryann managed to say.

"Thanks. I'll expect him later. Bye now," Linda said, and hung up.

Maryann just sat there for a little bit after

she put the phone back on its cradle. Finally, she looked up at Horace, the moose head, and asked him, "Well, what do you think of that? A dozen long stem red roses."

Of course, Horace never answered—and another phone call came in right away, so she tried to put the flowers out of her mind, too. After all, it was going to be a busy day, especially if she got the appointments back. She'd need to leave space for the meeting with Timmy, and then they'd want to close early tonight because of the choir rehearsal for the Christmas pageant. And at some time today— most likely after it was too late in the day to get anyone to fly them to Juneau—Rocco would tell his brother that he was in town.

Alex stopped at Lizbet's on his way to the office, just on the chance his flowers had come in. The diner didn't look as cozy in the daytime as it did at night. The outside paint was scuffed in places, and the porch tilted a little, maybe because it needed some work on the support beams.

The smell of coffee and fried bacon greeted him when he opened the door, though, and he rubbed his hands together, grateful for the warmth. He stood just inside and looked for Linda. She was in the corner, her order pad in her hand as she talked to the people at the far table. Since she was the one who handled the shipment coming in, he figured he needed to wait for her. He sat down at a side table.

"Coffee?" one of the other waitresses came up and asked.

"Please," he said, and she filled the cup in front of him.

He cradled the cup in his hand, wondering for the hundredth time since he'd woken up what was going on with his brother. When Rocco didn't answer the phone call last night, Alex had assumed his brother was already sleeping. But when he didn't answer this morning either, he began to worry. If his brother was sleeping that much, it must mean he was depressed. Maybe that's what Rocco had been trying to tell him—that he needed his brother to come and be with him. Alex would go, of course, regardless of how reluctant he was feeling.

"Here you are, Romeo," Linda said, as she came up to him carrying a large crystal vase filled with roses. "Whoever she is, she's one fortunate woman."

Linda handed him the roses and he took a deep breath of their scent. They were fragrant and full, their deep red sure to please. He set them on the table so he could pull out his wallet to pay for them.

"What do I owe you?" He took a sip of his coffee.

"Ninety-seven dollars even," Linda said. "I'll knock off the seven dollars if you tell me who they're going to."

Alex chuckled. "Are you gals betting again?"

Linda shrugged. "The days are long. Our feet hurt, so we put them up and talk about what we see. So what if we sometimes have a little competition to see who's right?"

Alex grunted in disbelief. "A *little* competition? That's like saying you serve a *little* cheddar on your double-double cheeseburger."

Alex pulled his wallet out of his pocket and began to count out bills. When he finished, he added another ten-dollar bill for a tip and said, "Thanks for the roses. Maybe someday I'll tell you who I gave them to—she's kind of private and shy though. I don't think she'd want everyone to know."

Linda scrutinized him as though he might have a name tattooed on his forehead. "I understand Delilah can seem shy to those who know her best."

"Delilah?" he asked. "The fancy woman? No, she's not the one."

Linda peered down at him. "Don't worry. I'll find out who she is. I already asked your nurse. She'll eventually tell me."

"Maryann?" Alex croaked out, as he half-rose from his chair. "What did you say to her?"

Linda's smile faded as realization struck her.

"Oh, I had no idea." She was silent for a moment and then she added, "You could tell a person, you know, before she steps in it."

"It's hopeless anyway," Alex muttered, as he sat back down. "I just wanted to go out in style, you know? Leave her some reason to think kindly of me in the future when I'm gone."

"She isn't going to think that kindly of you," Linda said, bracingly. "Not from just a bouquet of flowers, no matter how lovely they are. You need to romance her. With more than flowers. Maybe some music. And jewelry— nothing says 'remember me' better than a diamond bracelet."

"Diamonds?" Alex protested. "How much of a cut are you getting off those flowers anyway?

"I make a modest living," Linda said with dignity. "People give me tips all day long. Why not when I deliver something like this?"

"I'm not complaining," Alex said as he took a long sip of coffee. "I just mean, who has the money for diamonds?"

"You will, someday," Linda said. "You're a doctor. When you go down to Los Angeles, you'll make the big money."

Alex shrugged. "Medicine has never been about the money for me."

"Well, no one will blame you if that's what it becomes," Linda said. "We could use some of it around here."

With that, Alex drained his cup and stood up. "Thanks for getting the flowers." He picked up the vase.

"I hope they work for you," Linda said, with a smile. "I figure she'll probably remember you kindly no matter what."

He walked fast from the diner to his clinic. He had forgotten how cold it was out. The roses he was carrying weren't used to temperatures like these. He was relieved when he got to the door of the clinic without losing any leaves or petals. He put his hand on the cold metal of the doorknob and turned it. Maryann was standing facing the file cases where they kept their patient files. It had only been recently that he noticed how she always looked so fresh and calm. He supposed it was that she almost always wore the white nurse's uniform.

"I have Timmy scheduled for eleven o'clock," Maryann said, without turning around to look at him. "His father will bring him in."

"Good, I'll have to let Amy know."

"I already did," she said as she pulled out a file and closed the drawer. "In the meantime, you have an appointment coming at nine and one at nine-thirty. I'm still working on ten and ten-thirty."

Alex nodded.

That's when Maryann turned around. He saw the soft expression transform her face.

"For you," he said as he held out the vase to her.

She walked toward him. "Those are even more gorgeous than Linda said."

"I wanted you to like them," Alex said as she got close enough to take the flowers.

Maryann held the vase and buried her face in the roses. "They are wonderful."

"Good," Alex said in relief. He had wanted her to be pleased. "I hope you know how special I think you are. Not only as a nurse but also as a woman. If there was any way I could stay here with you—" He stopped before he started to tear up. "My brother needs me."

Maryann seemed to stiffen at his mention of Rocco.

"I know it might be old-fashioned to have that kind of a commitment to a brother," Alex said. "But Rocco saved my life. I owe him everything."

She seemed to soften at his words. "Maybe Rocco doesn't want you to owe him everything."

Alex shook his head. "I wish I could believe that. But right now he's sitting in our parent's house down there, so overcome with depression that he's sleeping his life away. I doubt he knows what he wants. I've tried calling him and no one ever answers."

"Oh," Maryann said as she looked up at him. "Maybe he's gone out or something?"

"Not Rocco."

"Have you ever asked him what he wants?" Maryann said as she turned to go back to her desk. "Maybe you should talk to him. He might surprise you."

Alex grunted. "I have to reach him on the phone first. He hasn't called here, has he?"

"Here?" Maryann repeated the word as she set the vase of roses on her desk. "No, he hasn't called here."

"It's not like him to miss my birthday," Alex said with a frown. "I wonder if I should have the police check the house and see that he's okay. I'd hate to think of him taking a fall in his wheelchair and lying there not being able to get to the phone or anything."

"I don't think you need to call the police yet," Maryann said.

Alex nodded. "Yeah, I suppose. After all, he does have that attendant. Maybe Rocco decided to try and go to the grocery store and I've just missed him. Why knows, maybe he even decided to wheel himself around the block and get some sunshine."

"I'm sure it's something like that," Maryann said as she walked around her desk and sat in her chair. She reached across her desk and adjusted the placement of the vase. "If you don't hear from him by tomorrow, then you can call."

"I guess," Alex said as he started walking back to his office. "Who's my first appointment?"

"The Hazzel baby. An earache. The poor thing," Maryann said. "The file's on your desk already."

Maryann held her feelings in check until she heard the door close on the back exam room where Alex had his office. Her heart had jumped when she saw the roses; she'd never expected a dozen such beautiful flowers. And just when she thought maybe he had feelings for her, too, he said he was leaving anyway. She would cry, but she couldn't even do that, because she was too upset.

Just then Mrs. Hazzel came in the door with her baby wrapped in a blanket, and Maryann tried to put her emotions on hold. The day had begun for the clinic. She was a professional and she couldn't lay her head down and cry. It wasn't easy, but Maryann alternated between calling patients to reschedule their appointments and assisting Alex in the exam room. It was ten forty-five before she knew it.

Maryann sat down at her desk to rest. She was staring at the vase of roses when Amy came into the clinic.

"I'm early," the red-haired woman said breezily as she stepped through the door. Then she looked at the flowers. "What gorgeous roses."

Amy walked over and took a deep breath of their fragrance. "Oh, that smells so good. How do you get any work done? I'd sit and look at them all day."

"I do admire them here and there," Maryann said, trying to match the other woman's enthusiasm. She should have stopped there,

but something in Amy's face promised understanding. "I only wish they were real."

Amy frowned and leaned closer. "They
look real to me."

Maryann tried to smile. "The roses are. The
sentiment isn't."

"Ah," Amy said as she stepped back and
then got a chair to pull over so she could sit
down beside Maryann's desk. "It's Alex, isn't
it?"

Maryann glanced back to be sure that the
exam door was shut. Their ten-thirty appointment had called to reschedule for this afternoon, so Alex was using the time to finish
some of his notes.

"I don't know if it's him or me," Maryann
admitted. "I'm all churned up inside, and I
don't like it. He gives me the flowers and I'm
all happy inside. Then he tells me he's leaving anyway, so I'm down. I think maybe we
can work it out long-distance, and all he can
talk about is his duty. I hate feeling this way.
I moved to Alaska to have peace of mind."

"Really?" Amy leaned back and looked
bemused.

"Yes," Maryann said emphatically. "And
I've done everything right. I went back to
church. I feel God so solid with me. I've been
praying. I clear my mind every night before

I go to bed so I can sleep peacefully. If I do what I know to do, I figure God should do the rest."

There was silence for a moment.

"So God is supposed to keep everything serene?" Amy asked.

"Well, yes," Maryann answered, relieved to finally say the words aloud to someone who would understand. Then she added, "You have to understand, in my family everyone seems to be so dramatic every time they fall in love. Drama in, hysteria out. And then it starts all over again. I thought here in Alaska—away from them—I could be my own person and have a relationship that is calm and orderly." She paused and then realized all she had said. "Not that Alex and I have a relationship. I mean he's leaving, it's just that…"

Her voice trailed off and she sat there, a ball of misery if there ever was one. Amy was so quiet Maryann started to worry she wasn't going to answer.

Then she did. "You remind me of myself when I first met Ben. Years ago. I was so scared, and I wanted everything to be perfect. It wasn't, of course. I suppose I could have blamed God for it, too, but…" Amy gave a wide grin to Maryann. "Forgive me for saying so, but God doesn't promise any of us a lack of pain and anguish. I think His peace is supposed to come in the bearing of our problems, not in the lack of them. We can't have a full life if we can't accept some drama in our emotions."

"Oh," Maryann said, as she looked at the other woman. "You're sure about this? Because I had my heart set on things being easier."

Amy smiled. "I'm sorry."

"You don't think Alex is going to stay here, do you?" she asked the other woman, not bothering to hide all of the yearning she'd recently discovered in her heart. "I didn't even know I cared until a couple of days ago."

"Caring is always a precious thing," Amy said softly. "And no, I don't know how it will turn out for you and him." The widow hesitated for a moment. "And even if you do marry, there are no guarantees you won't be parted."

"Oh, dear," Maryann realized who she was talking to about this. "I'm so sorry. I wasn't thinking."

"You don't need to apologize." Amy had a tear in her eye. "God and I are working on my peace just like He is working with you on yours. We all travel our own path with Him. I have noticed, though, that peace doesn't mean things are smooth."

Amy took Maryann's hand and pressed it. "I'll be praying for you."

"Thank you." Maryann nodded. "I'll do the same for you."

The two women sat together for a few moments in silence. Maryann wondered how she had missed seeing the difference between the kind of chaos that surrounded her parents and the kind of problems that were part of an authentic, deep life. She still wished someone could tell her whether to withdraw and shield herself from disappointment with Alex, or whether she should go forward and care about him more deeply, whether he could return her feelings or not.

Chapter Thirteen

Alex sat at his desk, his hands holding a medical journal and his mind not bothering to read any of the words in front of him. He'd caught Maryann looking at those roses when she didn't know he could see her, and he knew they made her sad.

Just then, there was a knock on the door and he put his journal down and straightened his lab coat. "Yes?"

Maryann opened the door. "The Fields family is here. Amy's out here, too."

"Why don't you give me a minute alone with the parents and then we'll talk to Timmy," he suggested.

Maryann nodded. "I'll tell them to come in."

Alex resisted the urge to tap his fingers against his desk. He hadn't quite figured out how to tell Mr. and Mrs. Fields he had paid the hospital bill. He hadn't considered their pride when he'd done it. Although he had no choice, not if Timmy had been going to get the care he needed.

"Ah, come in," Alex said as he stood up. Timmy's parents were standing in the open doorway, looking hesitant, so he added, "Please have a seat."

Alex decided he'd do better if he didn't sit behind his desk, so he moved his chair to the side of the desk and arranged the two office chairs across from him.

"Did you have a good drive into town this morning?" Alex asked the couple, as they were getting seated. He was babbling and he knew it.

Mr. Fields nodded politely. "The roads haven't been bad lately, and I got my pickup fixed."

"Good," Alex said as he sat down.

"I'm looking to get some work at the General Store with Harry," Mr. Fields said proudly. "He's changing out some of his stock, and he said he could use help two days a week."

"We're going to put every one of his checks towards that hospital bill, too," Mrs. Fields said, satisfaction marking her voice. "I don't want you to think we're not going to pay it off as fast as we can."

"'Course, I only have work through October," Mr. Fields admitted. "But it'll pay down a few hundred. That'll get us started."

Alex cleared his throat.

"About the hospital bill," he said and then paused. "The thing is—I paid it."

There was absolute silence in the room.

Mrs. Fields shook her head. "You mean you arranged for us to pay it?"

Alex shook his head. "No, I paid it. They wouldn't admit Timmy any other way."

"You saved our boy's life," Mrs. Fields said, and a tear rolled down her cheek.

"But we can't let him pay the bill," Mr. Fields protested, as he turned to his wife. His face was red, either with embarrassment or shock, Alex didn't know which. "What will people say when they know he paid it?"

"A doctor has a duty to his patients," Alex said, trying to explain.

"But the whole community is raising money to pay this bill," Mr. Fields said. "It's one thing to have everyone chip in a dollar or two. We do the same when someone else needs it. But to have you pay the whole thing—that's nothing but charity."

"I don't think I'd call it charity," Alex protested.

"It's not the way we do things up here," Mr. Fields said adamantly. "You wouldn't understand that, being an outsider, but we have our ways. And taking charity isn't one of them."

"I treated Timmy for you earlier," Alex said, confused now.

"But I'm building you those shelves," Mr. Fields said. "That's fair. But the hospital bill—I can't build anything to equal that. I'd have to put you up a skyscraper."

Everyone was silent for a moment.

"How much was the bill?" Mrs. Fields finally asked.

Alex told him.

"I thought they were giving us a discount," Mrs. Fields protested.

"That was with the discount," Alex said.

"We're going to have to tell people," Mr. Fields said. "At that pancake breakfast on Saturday, we'll have to get up in front and tell everyone Dr. Havens paid off the bill, so they can keep their money for another cause."

"I'd really rather you didn't mention my name," Alex said. "People don't need to know who paid it."

"Well, they would figure that out real fast without us saying your name anyway," Mr.

Fields said. "Who else was up in Juneau to do something like that? They know your nurse doesn't have that kind of money."

"It could have been Max," Alex said. Maybe his friend would enjoy the attention.

Mr. Fields shook his head morosely. "No, he wouldn't do something like this. He keeps all his money for those airplanes of his. Nobody would believe he'd pay for Timmy."

"You can say it was an anonymous donor," Alex pleaded. "People give money all the time, and don't want their names mentioned."

"They're going to think I robbed a bank or something," Mr. Fields said, fretting as he turned to his wife. "Or maybe they'll think I found that treasure that Amy's great-great-something buried all those years ago."

"I don't know—" Mrs. Fields began.

"Mark my words," her husband said, interrupting her. "People are going to be out at our place, digging holes all over, trying to find some of the treasure they think I have, if we don't tell everyone what happened."

"Well…" Alex said. He could see the other man wasn't going to wind down anytime soon. "Please just think about it. We have some time between now and Saturday."

"Thank you," Mrs. Fields said quietly as she stood up. "Maryann said you didn't need us when you talk to Timmy, so we'll wait outside. I have a few things to get at the general store, so we'll be back in a bit to pick up Timmy."

Alex nodded as he stood up. "That works very well."

He shook hands with the couple, and then they left the room.

He sat down. It was worse than he'd thought. He hadn't even begun to consider all of the complications if his role in paying Timmy's bill became known. It did mark him as an outsider. Not many people in this town had enough in savings that they could have paid the bill off completely.

It wasn't long before Amy and Timmy were standing in the open doorway. Amy was carrying the Bible that had the map inside of it.

"Maryann's not coming?" he asked.

Amy shook her head, but didn't offer any explanation.

Alex let Timmy sit in the chair for a bit before he began.

"How are you feeling?" he asked the boy. "Are you doing okay?"

Timmy nodded. He kept looking at that Bible. "I'm a little tired."

Alex didn't have the heart to chastise the boy, but it had to be done. Boys didn't grow to responsible men if they didn't face the consequences of their actions. If there was one lesson that had been seared on his heart, that was the one.

"We need to talk about the map," Alex said. There was no reason to delay. "Do you know who the map belongs to?"

Timmy nodded his head and gave a sideways glance at Amy. "It's hers."

"Okay then," Alex said. "What do you think you could do to make things right with Amy?"

Timmy looked up and scrunched up his face in thought. "I could give the map back."

Alex nodded, "That's the first step. What else?"

"I could find the treasure for her," Timmy said. His face lit up at this prospect. "I think I saw something when I was out there. Maybe we could go back and find it. I know just where to look."

"You're never to go back there alone." Alex kept his voice soft and tried not to show the panic he felt when he saw the excitement on the boy's face. "You need someone older to go with you. And not just another kid. An adult. Besides, I was thinking of something you could do to show Amy how sorry you are that you took something that belonged to her—nothing to do with the treasure."

Timmy thought some more, his face twisted in the effort. "I could give her my bike, but it lost a wheel, so it doesn't work too good."

"I think maybe a simple 'I'm sorry' will do," Amy said as she smiled down at the boy. "With a promise not to steal anything again."

Timmy's face brightened. "I *am* sorry, and I promise never ever to take anything that's not mine. Not ever again."

"Well, that settles it then," Amy said.

"No, I think he needs to do something to earn his forgiveness," Alex said. "Maybe he can help you in your garden for a couple of days. That's good hard work."

"It's September," Amy protested. "There's not much that's still growing."

"He could help you get the ground ready for next year," Alex said. He didn't want Amy to go to soft on the boy. Timmy's actions had serious consequences, and he needed to understand that.

"You don't mean digging up the dirt!" Amy looked shocked. "He's too young."

"He could help with the digging," Alex said. "Maybe move some of those rocks around to make a new border for your flower beds."

Alex looked over at Timmy. The boy was looking worried. "Of course, you'll need to wait until he's completely well."

"Can my friends help me?" Timmy asked.

"We'll talk about it later," Alex said. He was convinced the boy understood the gravity of his poor choices.

Timmy swallowed. "You're not going to tell my parents, are you?"

Alex wondered if everyone hadn't had enough emotion-packed confessions for the time being. "Not today. But you'll need to tell them yourself in a day or two."

"I'm sure they'll understand," Amy added. "If you want, you can have them call me and I'll tell them it's all right."

Alex frowned. "You mean, it will be all right when he helps you get the garden ready for next year?"

Amy frowned back at Alex before she turned to Timmy and smiled. "Just have them call me if they have any questions—"

Then Amy stood up and reached out for Timmy's hand. "I'm sure your parents want to get you home again. The day is nice right now, but it could turn cold again as the afternoon goes on."

Timmy stood up and took her hand.

"I'll talk to you later," Amy said to Alex and he figured she meant to tell him why he was wrong in suggesting Timmy help her with her garden to make amends for what he did. She didn't know, though, what guilt did to a man when he couldn't do anything to fix the things he'd done wrong in this life.

He knew Timmy was a young boy, but Alex hadn't been much older when the accident happened. It would have been helpful if someone older and wiser had been there to tell him it was good to do something hard and physical to show how sorry he was. Maybe then he could have found a way to actually say the words.

He listened until he heard the door outside close a few times. Then he went back to his journal.

Chapter Fourteen

Maryann knew from the darkness outside the clinic windows that it was past closing time, but she had postponed walking to the door and flipping the sign because she kept thinking Rocco would show up. She knew he wasn't accustomed to wheeling himself down rough asphalt roads, so she figured he might need extra time. She kept walking to the window to look outside toward the boarding house, but no one was coming down the road.

Her heart sank. The longer she had to hide what she knew from Alex, the worse she felt. She knew she hadn't lied to him about Rocco, but surely he deserved to know.

She had closed her eyes a few minutes ago, and prayed that Rocco would come; but the clock kept ticking, and he hadn't arrived.

Technically, she supposed, he had until midnight to tell Alex he was here, but it didn't seem likely Rocco could wheel himself down to his brother's place that late at night.

She glanced over at the vase of roses that stood on her desk. She couldn't even solve the problems *she* had; she shouldn't fret about other those of other people. She had run Amy's words round and round in her mind since they'd had their talk. Was she really trying to run away from all of the emotions of life? She wondered how to strike a balance in her feelings. Maybe she could feel the full range of emotions without exaggerating them, as her parents did.

She looked up when she heard Alex walking through the hall, coming toward the waiting room.

"Ready to go?" he said, when he got to her desk. "Amy's going to be calling the choir to order any minute now."

Maryann nodded as she stood up from her desk and reached for her jacket. "Are you taking your medical bag—since you're the doctor?"

"I've got it covered," he said with a grin as he pulled a packet of cough drops out of the pocket of his jacket.

Maryann smiled. "You might want to grab

another bag. I think you might have lots of singers coming to you for voice strain."

Alex lifted his eyebrow in a question.

"The fancy women," Maryann said. "They'll want to talk to you, and what better way than to say they have a sore throat from singing so much."

"You're probably right," he said as he turned to walk back to the exam room where they kept the supplies.

While he was doing that, Maryann decided to make a sign saying Dr. Havens was at the church. That way, if Rocco did want to see him tonight, he'd know where to look. She wrote the letters of her note in bold, black marker, and got out a piece of adhesive tape so she could be sure it stayed on the door.

"Expecting someone?" Alex asked as he came back and saw her taping the note to the door.

"You never know," she said.

Alex shrugged. "It's probably a good idea all right. There could be an emergency."

Once she had the sign posted, they turned off the inside light and closed the door. The faint light coming in from the nearest street lamp would be enough for someone to read the note without a flashlight.

They made their way down the porch steps.

Except for the circles of light from the street lamps, the night was dark. The sky had been overcast earlier, and the clouds must still be up there, because there were no stars showing. The air had a raw coldness to it that promised snow before too many more days.

Alex put his arm around her shoulders with a naturalness that indicated he thought it had become the way they walked together. She supposed that was true by now. She was determined not to try to avoid any feelings, so she didn't back away when Alex pulled her a little closer. She did not have many more night walks with him, and she'd want to remember them later.

Warm, yellow light streamed out of the windows of the Treasure Creek Christian Church. There were a dozen or so steps leading to the porch of this plain, white clapboard church, and a steep wheelchair ramp ran up the side. The most impressive thing about the church was its high steeple. Maryann had heard it said that the founders of Treasure Creek put up the tallest steeple they could find so miners could find their way to town when they were coming down from the mountains. Over the years, the church had expanded on its reputation for being a beacon to guide people home.

When they got to the top of the stairs, Alex reached for the door handle, but then drew his hand back and turned to her until both of his arms were on her shoulders. He was standing so close that his open jacket formed a cocoon of warmth and comfort with her in the center.

"Do we have to go inside?" he whispered.

"I—I don't know," she said, her heart thumping. She could see his face in the darkness—the line of his jaw, the half smile on his lips. "Amy is counting on us."

He nodded, but did not move. A minute passed.

Then he murmured, "Sometimes I get so tired of doing my duty. Even when I have to—even when people are counting on me."

Maryann nodded, but she didn't answer. She didn't know what to say to the yearning in his voice. His eyes were intent.

"I just want you to know I want to stay here with you. Even if I go, I want you to know I wish it were different."

Maryann felt hope rise up inside of her and then crash to the ground.

"Don't say that," she said, as she took a step back. "Not yet. Not until you talk to your brother."

It wasn't fair, she reminded herself, to let

him make any kind of declaration when he didn't know that his brother wasn't lying in bed in Los Angeles, barely able to move because of some great depression. It was easy for Alex to declare he wanted to stay when he knew he had to leave. But how would he feel if Rocco said he didn't need him, that Alex was free to live where he wanted?

"I just think you should wait a bit," she said when he didn't say anything more.

Finally, he nodded and reached for the door handle again. This time he opened it and waited for Maryann to enter first.

The sounds of talk and laughter drifted back to where they stood, in the shadows of the entryway.

Alex had never felt so alone. Not even after the accident. It didn't matter if Maryann stood by him or not. He needed to wait for a minute or two before he was ready to face the group of people who were getting ready to sing together. He had misread Maryann's feelings for him, that much was clear. He supposed in time he would feel mortified at how open he'd been with his own feelings when she did not share them. For now though, he was too numb to care.

"You go ahead," he finally had breath enough to say to Maryann.

"I—" she started.

But he shook his head. "We'll talk later."

He still couldn't turn and look at her, but he heard her take a first hesitant step away from him, so he added, "Please."

She would need to talk to him later, he knew. Nothing would be easy about this. She couldn't bear to hurt anyone. She'd want to bandage his wounds, and he would have to let her, listening to her say how sorry she was, and how he would find someone else and that he'd be happy in time. He knew she would have to say the words and he would have to listen, but he just couldn't do it yet.

He watched her walk down the aisle to the front of the church and stop to whisper something in Amy's ears. Then he saw the other woman look back to where he stood. Fortunately, Amy turned back to Maryann and nodded. Then Maryann kept walking— and slipped out the door at the side of the church.

Alex needed to sit down, so he walked to the last pew. He sat down and leaned forward until his head rested on the top of the pew in front of him. For the first time since he was a boy, he started to pray. He had no fine words to say, he just knew he needed mercy. The chasms between him and the people he loved were too deep for him to cross alone.

He sat there for a long time, the people in the front of the church managing to sing through the whole song of "Amazing Grace." He'd never known it to be a song used in a Christmas pageant, so he figured Amy was trying to comfort him as best she could.

And then he felt a firm hand on his shoulder. He looked up to see Reverend Michaels, middle-aged and kind, sit down next to him on the pew.

"Can I help?" the man asked softly.

Alex looked up and tried to smile. "Not unless you have a 'Get Out of Jail Free' card."

Reverend Michaels grinned. "Actually, I have something that works even better."

Alex expected the reverend to start preaching at him with that, but the man just sat and let his presence be comforting. They were quiet together for a few minutes.

"I guess I have a problem," Alex finally said. "At least Amy thinks I do. I've always thought a man should make amends for what he's done to hurt others. Even a boy like Timmy Fields needs to learn to make amends. How else do you show someone you're sorry?"

The reverend nodded. "And that's what you're trying to do, too, I'm guessing."

Alex nodded. "It's killing me."

"God knows a man's heart," Reverend Michaels said. "He knows who is repentant. I noticed you were praying."

Alex nodded. "Praying, but not believing He'd answer. And why should He? I've let Him down, too."

The reverend was quiet for so long Alex thought he had discouraged the man. Then he spoke again.

"How would you like that 'Get Out of Jail Free' card?" he asked. "To have a new start, where someone else paid your amends for every failure in your life? Where you were forgiven for every bad thing you did and every good thing you failed to do?"

"I don't think it's that easy," Alex said.

The reverend smiled. "God says it is."

Alex closed his eyes. No one needed to connect any more of the dots. But did he dare risk believing God would do that for him? He felt the ice inside him start to melt. He had to believe.

When he opened his eyes, he faced the reverend squarely and nodded.

Just then, he noticed the church had become very quiet. He looked up toward the front and saw that Amy had walked closer to him. The others were up there, standing still and watching as if they were expecting something to happen.

The double door to the church opened and a man walked in.

"Nate? Nate McMann?" Amy said as she hurried down the aisle. "You're just the man I wanted to see. I thought you were still out on that fishing boat."

Nate grinned at her. "I had to come back to see what people were up to here. Why?"

"I just thought you might want to help lead a tour for me," Amy said.

Alex recognized the matchmaking look on Amy's face, but he didn't think the other man did. He wondered who the tour boss had in mind for the man.

"Sounds great," Nate said, then he looked around. "I saw the lights on here, so I came on over. It's a good thing, too. I needed to help someone outside."

"Oh, we forgot about the ramp," Amy exclaimed as she continued toward the door. "I should have sent someone with her."

Nate reached the door ahead of her. "I was just giving them a minute to get ready for their entrance."

Alex had the strangest sensation that they

were talking about Maryann and someone. But he couldn't figure out what all the secrecy was about. Then he remembered she'd had something she couldn't tell him.

Nate opened one side of the double door while Amy opened the other and Alex felt his world spin. The entryway to the church wasn't well lit, and the man in the wheelchair was still on the porch outside in the dark, so Alex couldn't see his face yet. But he recognized the heft of the shoulders and the tilt of the head.

"Rocco?" he whispered.

Maryann stood to the side of where Rocco sat in his wheelchair, getting ready to go inside the church. He had come so far, he deserved to make the final few yards of the journey alone. She had prayed with him before he'd maneuvered himself squarely in front of the door. Then she stepped aside.

She looked at the astonishment on Alex's face. She could almost see him putting all of the pieces together and trying to find answers to his question as Rocco slowly wheeled himself inside the entryway of the church and faced him.

"Where's that attendant of yours?" Alex finally managed to say. "He should know better than to bring you this far. I can't believe—"

Alex stood up and started to walk to the door, like he was going to search outside for the man.

"He's in Denver," Rocco said calmly. "Visiting a niece."

If Alex could look more shocked, he did. "Then who? Surely our parents didn't—"

Rocco laughed as he wheeled himself further inside. "Not likely."

Alex stopped and stared at his brother. Finally, he demanded to know, "Then who?"

Rocco sat up straighter in his wheelchair. "Me. I brought myself here."

"But you won't even go to the grocery store," Alex protested weakly. "How?"

Maryann hugged herself when she saw the look on Alex's face. He did not like to be unprepared. Every square needed to be placed just so for a plan to work in his mind. Maybe he truly had meant what he'd said earlier about wanting to be with her, but not knowing how the squares would all fall into place had meant he couldn't commit to more than the feeling.

"I've been practicing and working out,"

Rocco said proudly. "The attendant you hired showed me how. I do pretty good now."

Alex finally sat down again, this time in a straight back chair that had been set beside the coat rack for when people needed to take off their boots. "But why didn't you tell me you were coming?"

Maryann watched the brothers.

Rocco rolled closer and sat eye-to-eye with his brother. "You would have told me not to come. You would have said you have a duty to give me this or build me that. I wanted to come and see a live moose. And see the mountains I've heard about. And eat the apple pie at the diner. "

Alex looked at his brother for a long time before he smiled. "And have you eaten some apple pie? And seen a moose?"

Rocco shook his head and grinned. "Not yet. That moose hasn't been in town since I've been here, and I wanted to take you with me to get the apple pie."

"Well, we've got time," Alex said as he reached over and hugged his brother. When he pulled away, he asked. "How long are you staying, anyway?"

Rocco looked away at that one. For the first time, Maryann sensed that Rocco needed some help. She walked in and squatted by his wheelchair. He nodded gratefully to her and then turned to Alex. "I thought I might— well, you see Lindy offered me a job and— the maid's quarters are pretty comfortable. It might take some time to actually see a moose."

Maryann noticed that Alex was now looking at her.

"You knew all of this," Alex said, his voice flat. "This is what you couldn't tell me."

Maryann nodded. She was miserable, but she'd not lie.

"You didn't—" Alex started and then stopped.

She knew what he meant, and she shook her head. "I didn't even know he was here until I saw him at Lindy's when I got back from Juneau."

"She worried the whole time about how you would take it," Rocco added softly. "I'm the one who asked her not to tell you. I was afraid you'd make me leave before I got a chance to look around."

Alex stood then, and walked toward her. She couldn't read his expression, but she thought he looked nervous. She'd never seen that look on his face before. He appeared very uncertain,

"Is that why you didn't want me to continue earlier?" he asked softly.

Maryann looked around her and saw the church was empty, except for the three of them. Amy must have ushered the others out the side door.

She nodded. "I thought you shouldn't say anything until you knew."

She heard Rocco wheeling his chair to the front of the church.

Alex grinned. "Then let me tell you again. I want to stay with you. Here in Treasure Creek. I want us to walk with each other and God here, in this place. I know it's too soon to talk of marriage, but I figure, in a week or so I'll have earned the right to ask you to marry me."

"Yes," Maryann said.

Alex drew in a quick breath. "When you say 'yes,' is that 'yes, I'll have earned the right to ask'? Or 'yes that'—"

She stood there in the entryway to the church and watched the hope build in his eyes. His hand reached out to smooth back her hair, and she reached up to touch his cheek just for the pleasure of it.

"We should probably go on a few dates before I say yes," she finally said. She took a deep breath. "Just so we know for sure."

"I forgot," Alex said, with a smile. "You want to make your decision based on logic, wasn't it? Genes and common sense and—"

Alex's voice trailed off, and he looked at her for a long moment before bending down to kiss her.

Maryann's head swirled.

"We can go on a hundred dates," he whispered, after that. "I love you and already know for sure you're the one for me. I want you to feel the same. What is it you Jenners need? To be poleaxed by love?"

"I'm immune to that," she murmured, as he kissed her again.

Epilogue

A few months later, when winter had firmly taken hold of Treasure Creek, Maryann and Alex were married in the old Russian church. The city had decided to sell the building, and Alex had purchased it for his new clinic, with the understanding that he would preserve the historic building and let tourists gawk at it as often as they wanted. There would be enough room for all the new equipment he wanted for his practice, and Alex liked the image of healing the sick in a house of worship.

Maryann now stood at the end of the aisle, waiting for the processional to begin. The fragrance of the fresh red roses in her bouquet mingled with that of wax. Mr. Fields had worked for days, buffing and polishing the old wood floor until it shone. The light coming through the windows on the sides of the church showed it off beautifully.

There had not been enough chairs for all of the people who wanted to come, so Lizbet's Diner closed for the day, and Max had hauled all of their chairs over in his pickup.

Maryann marveled at the community of friends she had here. The Reverend Michaels had happily agreed to conduct the service, and people had came from all around to see their doctor marry his nurse. The Fields family was proudly sitting in the front row.

The music finally began and her maid of honor, Karenna, started down the strip of carpet that been laid down the aisle. Then it was time for Maryann to walk toward Alex. It wasn't until she was halfway down, looking into his eyes the whole way, that she started to feel a little faint and couldn't quite catch her next breath. Then the butterflies in her stomach increased their flutter and she gripped her bouquet tighter before swaying a little. And then her knees felt funny, as if they were made of Jell-O.

The next thing Maryann knew she was lying on the carpet with Alex kneeling beside her, taking her pulse and smoothing back her hair.

"What's wrong?" The reverend was standing

there, staring down with a worried look on his face.

Karenna started to chuckle as she bent over and winked at Maryann, and then Alex joined in.

"She's been poleaxed by love," Karenna said as she straightened up. "It's a family trait, and it's about time, if you ask me."

"I wasn't—" Maryann started to protest, but then she looked up at Alex and grinned. The man did have a powerful effect on her. Maybe it wasn't so bad to feel all of her emotions after all. "You know, I think Karenna's right."

Alex's grin turned triumphant.

Then he leaned down and kissed her.

* * * * *

Dear Reader,

I still remember my first view of the mountains in Alaska. I was sitting in the copilot seat of a small plane, and the view was absolutely breathtaking. Those mountains are majestic. And it isn't just the scenery that makes it a great state. My impression of the people of Alaska is that they are rugged individuals—just the kind of people, like Alex, who would put everything on the line to save a small boy's life.

As you can tell, I was ready to revisit the state through my imagination, so I was delighted to join the other authors in this series as we figured out how to tell the story of a small tourist town and the treasure map they sought.

Of course, each book is different in the series and I was fortunate enough to be assigned the story of Alex and Maryann—a doctor and a nurse, both committed to taking care of others, even when they don't always take the best care of themselves. Alex had made a mistake as a child and is planning to make amends by building a medical clinic in his brother's name. Together Alex and Maryann discover that God is bigger than all their mistakes and plans. I hope you enjoy their story.

If you have a minute, I would love to hear from you. Just go to my Web site at www.janettronstad.com and e-mail me from there. In the meantime, God bless you and keep you.

Sincerely,

Janet Tronstad

QUESTIONS FOR DISCUSSION

1. Dr. Alex Havens had his life all planned—
   he was going to build a clinic—and then
   he found out that God had something else
   in mind for him. Do you believe Christians should even bother making plans?
   Do you make them?

2. Maryann Jenner raced up to Alaska
   because she was worried about her
   cousin. She obviously acted quickly and
   didn't make much of a plan. Are you
   more like her or Alex? How so? Do you
   think God has a preference for planners
   or impulsive people?

3. Can you name a character in the Bible
   who planned and one who didn't?

4. The fancy women had a plan, as well.
   They came up to Alaska in response
   to a magazine article that spoke of the
   bachelor tour guides. The desire of their
   hearts was to get married. We know God
   cares about the desires of our heart, but
   He does not always answer these prayers
   the way we want Him to. What do you

say to people who are disappointed that their prayers are not answered the way they want?

5. Even little Timmy had a plan. He was going to find the treasure so his parents would be happy. His parents were stressed because of finances. What stresses do you have in your life? How do you think these stresses affect the people around you? What would you say to parents like Timmy's whose stress affects their children?

6. Alex made his plans because of the guilt he felt for what had happened many years ago when his brother was crippled saving his life (when Alex wasn't being obedient). Have your actions ever caused someone to be hurt? Did you feel guilty for this? How did you respond?

7. Alex had told his brother he was sorry, but Alex didn't feel words were enough. That's why he wanted to build the clinic in his brother's name. Do you think there are times when "I'm sorry" isn't enough? Under what circumstances?

8. Did Alex go overboard in deciding to build the clinic? Why or why not?

9. Have you ever been hurt by someone's actions and they then tried to do something big to make it all better? Do you think a big gesture does make it better? When does it and when does it not?

10. Maryann moved to Alaska partly because she was tired of the chaos of her parents' lives. Different people are able to handle more chaos than others. Where do you fall on the spectrum?

11. The town Treasure Creek plays a big part in this series. Would you like to live in a place like Treasure Creek? Why or why not?

12. Is the town different from what you imagined Alaska to be like? If so, how?

13. One of the delightful things in this series is the treasure map. The prospect of finding unexpected treasure cheers up most people. Have you had a time in your life when you thought you might get an unexpected treasure? What happened?

14. If you (like the author of the treasure map) were going to leave something to your descendants, what would it be?

15. At this point in the series, do you have any guesses as to what the treasure is?

LARGER-PRINT BOOKS!

GET 2 FREE
LARGER-PRINT NOVELS
PLUS 2 FREE
MYSTERY GIFTS

Love Inspired®

Larger-print novels are now available...

YES! Please send me 2 FREE LARGER-PRINT Love Inspired® novels and my 2 FREE mystery gifts (gifts are worth about $10). After receiving them, if I don't wish to receive any more books, I can return the shipping statement marked "cancel". If I don't cancel, I will receive 6 brand-new novels every month and be billed just $4.74 per book in the U.S. or $5.24 per book in Canada. That's a saving of over 20% off the cover price. It's quite a bargain! Shipping and handling is just 50¢ per book.* I understand that accepting the 2 free books and gifts places me under no obligation to buy anything. I can always return a shipment and cancel at any time. Even if I never buy another book, the two free books and gifts are mine to keep forever.

122/322 IDN E7QP

Name _____ (PLEASE PRINT) _____

Address _____ Apt. # _____

City _____ State/Prov. _____ Zip/Postal Code _____

Signature (if under 18, a parent or guardian must sign) _____

Mail to Steeple Hill Reader Service:
IN U.S.A.: P.O. Box 1867, Buffalo, NY 14240-1867
IN CANADA: P.O. Box 609, Fort Erie, Ontario L2A 5X3

Not valid to current subscribers to Love Inspired Larger-Print books.

Are you a current subscriber to Love Inspired books
and want to receive the larger-print edition?
Call 1-800-873-8635 or visit www.morefreebooks.com.

* Terms and prices subject to change without notice. Prices do not include applicable taxes. Sales tax applicable in N.Y. Canadian residents will be charged applicable provincial taxes and GST. Offer not valid in Quebec. This offer is limited to one order per household. All orders subject to approval. Credit or debit balances in a customer's account(s) may be offset by any other outstanding balance owed by or to the customer. Please allow 4 to 6 weeks for delivery. Offer available while quantities last.

Your Privacy: Steeple Hill Books is committed to protecting your privacy. Our Privacy Policy is available online at www.SteepleHill.com or upon request from the Reader Service. From time to time we make our lists of customers available to reputable third parties who may have a product or service of interest to you. If you would prefer we not share your name and address, please check here. ☐

Help us get it right—We strive for accurate, respectful and relevant communications. To clarify or modify your communication preferences, visit us at www.ReaderService.com/consumerchoice.

LILP10R

SUSPENSE

RIVETING INSPIRATIONAL ROMANCE

Watch for our new series of
edge-of-your-seat suspense novels.
These contemporary tales
of intrigue and romance
feature Christian characters
facing challenges to their faith...
and their lives!

NOW AVAILABLE IN REGULAR
& LARGER-PRINT FORMATS

Steeple
Hill®

Visit:
www.SteepleHill.com

INSPIRATIONAL HISTORICAL ROMANCE

Engaging stories of romance,
adventure and faith,
these novels are set in
various historical periods
from biblical times
to World War II.

NOW AVAILABLE!

Steeple
Hill®